In The Days Of Jael

I see you. Not in a dream, as I don't sleep, except when the fever hits and I am unconscious with my life raging before me – small snippets in black and white – fast reels running at one hundred miles an hour. I'm here in Mayo in the cottage. I'm dying of cancer and Covid. I have this fancy that I'm here to finish my novel before I die. I am mixed up now, between you and Jael. Which one of you is real? Which one of you did I imagine? I think of the story that Murt told. You know, the one about your first pint in Mckenna's bar, down the side street near Murdock's? You not long out of short pants, catching the blaze of sunlight on a dusty trail leading to your pint of ale. Now, be assured, Dessie, that I am allowing you into my head. My thoughts are open to you, just for a little while.

Kate

Some nights, I imagine the sea crashing through the stone barriers at the top of the beach, flooding the road as it winds its way along to reach me. I'm not afraid of it at all as it merges with the calmer waters of Mullaghroe, where Grandad lost the beach ball. I nearly drowned retrieving it. Such a dressing down he gave me: "Yah nearly lost your life, girl, for a bag of air."

That was a year or two before he lost it. He was clear and lucid then but all through our evening meal, he kept repeating "A bag of air.". It became an incantation. I was thinking, if he could remember his rosary as well, but he stopped all that, too, well before he went mad, like, completely mad. The people around our place in Dublin thought he was odd all his life. Grandad lived in his own little bubble, his life bordered by his job on the buses, his music, and his religion.

In the evenings, when Dessie was doing his homework in the sitting room, Grandad would sit by the fire, a faint smell of diesel from his uniform, and recite stories from the bible. And sometimes he would pick up his thick copy to check that he'd delivered it properly. He was a great believer in accuracy and he told me and Dessie regularly that he hated spoofs. He kept the best stories 'til Dessie had his homework done, parking us both on the two-seater before reading for hours 'til we were tired of it. I wanted him to stop but I daren't ask as he had a vicious temper. He was always waiting to read his favourite lines before he got tired himself. Sometimes he got so carried away, he cried when he read his chosen passage. If we were truly exhausted, Dessie and I would cry, too, partly just to join him so he wouldn't feel alone but, more often, just with relief that the ordeal was at an end.

I can see Jack Oliver's face. He is standing at the end of the bed, his tiny frame, with his nose pulled out from his face, as if done with a plunger. As always, he is smiling. I tell myself that Jack Oliver didn't die, that he didn't get pancreatic cancer and die within a year, aged sixty-seven. He looks at me, perplexed. This is his place, and there I am lying in the same bed that he once lay in. I too have cancer, and I'm pretty sure I've Covid as well. I'm dying, so soon I will follow him, my boss of thirty years.

Mr Oliver, my kind benefactor of all those years, rewarded me with weekend trips to this place and a walk along Mullaghroe with Dessie. Then he brought Bridie, and more recently he came on his own, but this time it is different – I spend my days wishing, wishing I could wipe away those days and weeks with a cloth; give them a good old dusting down. My strength has left me. When I came back here, I walked the beach at Mullaghroe, then drove down to the Atlantic side, wanting to feel the wind on my face and the chill in the air.

I have few memories of Grandad on the Atlantic side. I had to drag him there as he said he couldn't sit and watch or be comfortable. No, he much preferred the calm of Mullaghroe. I love the wild side. As I search out over the white rollers, I get a view of Inishkea Island and dream about the old whaling station and the abandoned works belonging to it. When you're in Mayo, you know the next stop is America. Nobody has to convince you of that – it's plain to see how that vast ocean must lead somewhere. When I look out over the waves, I see little men loading ships on the quays of Boston and New York, and it is a great pity that I never went there, not even on a visit, like a long weekend, which has become fashionable now amongst the yuppies and the go-getters. My generation missed out on all that. My grandad never left Ireland, although he was a geographical genius. There was nothing he couldn't learn or didn't know about the wide world, and not just its geography but its history, or at least the version of history he learned.

He'd sit by Oliver's fire and get me to ask him questions, like the capital of this or about the longest rivers or the highest mountain, then he'd turn to Ireland and name all the mountain ranges throughout the country 'as Gaelige', as he swore that was the way he was taught them and he didn't know their names in English. Sitting there by the hearth, his favourite place, smoking a fag, his big bald football head down, he'd look up and frown, then bellow out "Sliabh Bladhma." Dessie threw his eyes to heaven and remarked sarcastically, "Well, that only took an hour," and Grandad laughed and said, "You needn't bother if you don't want to do it right."

Dessie, feeling sorry for him, took him outside and they walked down the lane to Mullaghroe beach, moving so slow because Grandad's legs were giving out – a dozen nervous cows watching them. Dessie chatted to him, all cheerful. From the window, I could see him pointing to the sky.

It's the warmest day of the year but I still light the fire – the same fire where Grandad warmed his arse all those years ago, sitting on the hearth when he finally told me about my parents. He did it upside down and arseways; he was never good on sentiment or tact. No. he barked it out, lost in a shade of embarrassment that contradicted his wisdom and world weariness. It was probably the only time I saw the little boy in him, and it was really magical and frightening to see him like that, for, despite his imperfections and true excesses, his vulnerability added to him, in my humble estimation, and this peek at his humanity allowed my empathic juices to flow.

"It was yer father's idea," he said, picking up the poker and rattling the whitish-looking cinders until they glowed bright orange. "Ida had nerves; you know." He lay the poker down and put his hands out to feel the brazen heat of the cinders. "Is it too late to put another log on? Are we gonna have another cuppa?"

I nodded and he picked a small log from the stack and placed it at the back of the grate. It caught straight away, and I felt sure I could feel it warm my insides.

"He took her to Killarney because she wanted to go up to Lady's View. Her mother had raved about it when she was alive, the poor woman never letting up about her one and only journey to Kerry. They stayed in this guesthouse out near Muckross, not far from the lakes. Ida was delighted with herself, and your father was convinced he was doing the right thing bringing her to Killarney. He told me before he left that the train journey itself might give him an opportunity to talk sense to her.

It happened all of a sudden. A month or so after Dessie was born, she changed. Mrs Stubbs said she was different when she came home from the hospital. She said she had a different look on her face than the one she had when she went in. I Dunno if they ever got to Lady's View but, that first night, the rear of the guesthouse went up in flames and they both died of smoke inhalation. Yer father was asleep in his bed and yer mother was found on the floor near the door, like she'd tried to get out but didn't make it. Funny how the front of the guesthouse was untouched. That was it. They were gone, and only for Mrs Stubbs, I'd have lost you and Dessie, and God knows."

He went for the poker and started to mess with the log, making sure to burn the back of it, so I went and made some tea. When I gave it to him, he sat there, all quiet, with his head bowed.

Whatever about Grandad and his silences, Dessie was his favourite. He was everyone's favourite, and for all that he was four years younger than me, he took charge like he was a great deal older. He was a beacon of responsibility, and even when he was in the midst of his alcoholism, he was always looking out for me and whoever his latest partner in life's crusade happened to be. It wasn't obvious to outsiders but, as Grandad faded with age, he lost control and Dessie went wild. I was born in 1955 – Dessie in '59 – so I spent my childhood minding him. In turn, he spent his adulthood watching out for me, when he could, although his alcoholism nearly did for both of us, and Grandad became oblivious to him. The world became a tiny bubble of fear for the old man, and he just couldn't keep up with it no matter how he tried.

It was grand when we were kids, when Grandad rented these old caravans in the wilds of West Cork, or later over near Ballinskelligs in Kerry. Those were the days when he drove his old Austin A 40 like a race car up and down boreens. He might read from his bible, alright, but he had his naggins hidden, and wasn't averse to leaving us in the caravan and driving to the Grange pub for some black pints. But during the day, he was great, bringing us to Dunworley and Ballinglanna, picking up stones and writing his name and our names and putting the date on them. I still have five or six of them in my room in the top drawer.

I never knew if Dessie was having a good time or not because he never said. He sort of laughed when he was meant to laugh and cried when he fell and scraped his hands or knees. He never said much and never really complained. I watched him running through the jagged rocks at Dunworley, his feet sinking in the wet sand, and he would dare the big waves to knock him over, screaming, "Come on, yah fucker!", and he was only eight years old. What an attitude. I was changing and I wanted no part of it. I'd go and grab his hand and whisper to him to watch his language or Grandad wouldn't go down to the Grange and leave us in the dark. If he heard the bad language, he would give us a lashing from the bible that wasn't to be challenged.

Dessie measuring up to the sea was a sight. The huge dark Atlantic wasn't tough enough for him, swearing at it, using his fists. Bring it on!

One good thing that Grandad made sure of was to stop at fields where he spotted horses, and one day, after Dunworley, he stopped at this field near Butlerstown, where a single horse stood, his head bent, chewing blades of grass. We stood at the gate, making sounds and rattling Grandad's car keys against the steel bars. The horse didn't pay a blind bit of attention to our antics. Then Dessie climbed on the gate and sat with his legs dangling on the field side. The horse became alert and cantered over, stopping about a yard away. His coat had this magnificent blue sheen, with a leather dazzle. Dessie held his hand out and the horse feigned to come forward but stopped and groaned, signalling that he was anxious. Grandad stepped away to light his pipe, then the horse stepped forward, right up to Dessie, and put his head against his right dangling leg. Dessie patted him on the mane and told him he was a good boy. The horse rubbed himself off Dessie's other leg, then rested his head between his legs. Grandad came back to the gate, his pipe in his right hand, and the horse withdrew, grunting, and I could see Dessie marvel at the beast, at his magnificence; his blueness, his shrewdness, and that's when he turned to me and said, "When I grow up, Kathy, I'm gonna be a horse," and even Grandad laughed at that.

The fire is burning, and the sun is blinding. I wish I had the strength to go down the beach or take the jeep to the Atlantic side. I'm burning with so much mental energy, just thinking about stuff and me writing this book that I may never finish. Where are they now? I know they stopped in Dunworley. Dessie loves it there, but did he pass the small triangular field where the old, battered caravan was? The last time I was down that way, the grass was all churned up and two frozen donkeys sheltered under the old tree that shaded the corner. It was easier to miss the poor creatures, but the caravan was long gone. Maybe he went round by the blue house along the quiet road 'til he took the twists and turns that brought them to Ballinglanna, that mystical headland that was spoiled with poorly built summer homes that people rent. The sprinkling of houses, the rocky beach, the polluted stream that makes its way home to Mother. I love the old walls, built solid like someone once had great plans for the place but for some reason changed their mind, yet still left those walls behind them. Grandad didn't like it there. He didn't like the flies that live amongst the weed and the stones. One day, he found some tin cans and plastic bottles in the stream. I told him they were just discards from passing ships. Another time, we found a lifebuoy and some empty plastic shampoo bottles. You could see how it could happen as the waves murdered the rocks, torturing them first with a mighty spray. Yet the water's edge at the little stone beach was calm enough, like the sea gave up when it got in that far.

Dessie liked to stand there and stare at the black water, like he was seeing stuff that the rest of us couldn't see. One day, this man stood right in Dessie's spot at the water's edge. Like Grandad, he smoked a pipe. Then we noticed a skinny runt of a boy wading in the waves about ten feet out. He looked nervous, scanning the cliffs and fields, the laneways, and roads. Beyond him, the roar of the Atlantic made him shivery and uncomfortable. The man watched over him, and every so often he'd take a puff of his pipe. The boy stood in three feet of the Atlantic Ocean. Then Dessie kicked up a fuss, as he wanted to wade in. I guess he wanted to put that skinny runt of a boy to shame but Grandad wouldn't let him as we forgot to bring a towel and he was one for picking up summer colds and temperatures, and sometimes he'd get so hot he'd start raving. You wouldn't put odds against him passing out.

I see the van struggling up the steep hill, with Dessie revving the accelerator. It's such a steep hill leaving Ballinglanna, no matter which way you go, back towards Barryroe or Dunworley, or the other way up past the grotto and on towards Ring. My gaze follows them like I'm a gliding bird, or one of those drones. I much prefer to follow Dessie and Jael, as the rest of the world is sick. Each night, I watch the images of our soon to be Taoiseach, Richard Fanon. His face pops up everywhere and I've christened him 'the laughing man', for no matter what question is put to him, he smiles. It could be about a nuclear bomb falling on a village in sub-Saharan Africa, he would still smile. His smile is near-permanent, and his only other face is a grimace, like when the socialists pull him up on some other crime against the poor. I can't stand him, his cheeky face, or his voice, so the sound stays turned down. It is my editing power to silence him, to mute his poison.

I'm forever eager but perhaps I need my bed to lie down, secure the fire, and ignore the sun. It was on these kinds of days that Grandad sent me to Mr Bowers with a note. This big dark, fat, hairy man would let me sit on the sofa of his living room while he went to his shed to get Grandad's order of stolen tobacco. Mr Bowers' three sons were in and out of jail regularly, and it was a given that one or other would be incarcerated. The mother was a morose, nervous sort who took to her bed in times of trouble, so was always in bed.

Bowers came back with the tobacco and stood over me like he'd never seen me before.

" Yah can tell him I haven't got that one, but we will get it again." He pointed to some tobacco brand I'd never heard of. "Yah should be getting old enough," he said, sitting beside me, and I moved to allow more room as I didn't want to touch him. When he turned towards me, I could see his yellow teeth, and his moustache was dirty, with bits of food and some traces of egg yolk. "Yah are old enough now." He put his hairy hand on my knee.

"I best be goin'. Grandad needs his tobacco."

He made no effort to stop me, though he followed me to the door, smirking as I looked back at him before starting to run for home.

2

The rain falls on the Western Road, and Jael is hit with flying jagged spears, the drops blue against the background of neon. Cars with tinted windows skid on the corner coming from the Mardyke and, in the distance, thunder rolls and sheets of lightening stab the sky. She glimpses dark cloud straying, enduring sky seizures. The blue rain pelts off the road and passing cars swish water up over the ridge of the path, hitting her feet and splashing her knees. A lorry sprays her midriff and she's soaked but she keeps her thumb up, then snaps it down as a single-decker bus pulls into the stop. It creates a tiny tsunami that drowns her feet again. As it pulls away, it absorbs some of the puddle, which ripples back towards her as the rear wheels search to grip the drier road. When it disappears, she sticks her thumb up once again, with several cars whizzing past. The rain hits her face and enters her eyes, warming as it bleeds down her soft skin. A white van pulls over. It's one of those new types she doesn't know the name of, and its wipers are on full, making a repeated menacing sound in the night air, so loud they are audible above the lashing rain. The driver leans over and opens the passenger door.

Jael looks him up and down.

The man is impatient, with the rain wetting the seat and floor, and the wipers still beating fast.

She climbs in. The strap of her rucksack slips and it falls to the floor between her legs.

'You shoulda put it in the back.'

She looks at him again, seeing him better now. He's in his late fifties, his hair too long for a man balding on top. He wears cheap glasses and adjusts them with his right hand as he peers into his side mirror before taking off.

'Where are you goin'?' he barks, but it isn't an angry bark – he's trying to be heard above the noise of the wipers.

Jael stops looking at him, distracted by the queue of traffic heading to the Wilton Roundabout. They are well back, with the cars ahead stopped solid.

'Where are you goin'?' she asks.

'You don't wanna know.'

'Oh. 'She smiles. 'Me too.'

'It's like that, is it? Fuckin' traffic is crap. It's the rain. Irish people don't handle extreme weather. Rain or snow, the whole fuckin' thing stops.' He pretends to study the rain hitting the windscreen.

The cars ahead start to inch forward. He puts both hands on the wheel and moves on about ten yards, then clicks the switch to put the wipers on a slower setting as the rain fades to a drizzle. The windscreen fills with water and Jael can't see until he switches the wipers back to fast for a few seconds and the screen clears again.

'Fuckin' rain, it's always rainin' in Cork.'

She laughs. 'No its not. I got sunburn last summer down by the river.'

'One day a year,' he says

The sun was razor sharp – its heat clung to her skin like it was made of tiny pieces of adhesive glass. Attracta watched the rowers pass, all young men with burly shoulders, wearing tight vests and grunting at each other in some strange guttural language. She smiled and touched Jael's shoulder, watching the foam swim away from the boat as the oars sunk deep and then splashed back to the surface. With one big grunt, the boat quickened and soon she was looking at their sturdy backs.

'I'd love to be fit,' she said, lolling her head back to allow the sun bake her skin.

'You used to be.'

'I was, but motherhood does that to a woman.'

Jael sighed. A wandering breeze swept down the harbour and a few people close by reached for cardigans, though

they just hung them over their shoulders, their instinct
telling them it was rogue and wouldn't last.
Her mother was fixated on the water, watching its deep
flow. To break the trance, she reached in her bag for her
cigarettes and lit one, blowing the smoke downwind.
Jael studied her. Attracta was ageing. Her face had
narrowed and her chin was pointing southwards but it was
her dark eyes that were once her beauty, now sunken in a
deep crevice of rich blood and roadmaps leading to the
core. The days and nights of drinking, the episodes of lying
on the floor, the crash-bang injuries: broken wrists;
broken arms; smashed heads; congealed blood; and long
days in bed. That smell, it stuck to her like some evil
demon had entered her room one night and sprayed her
with a demonic perfume. It was ever present and stayed on
her skin despite washing in suds and scrubbing with a nail
brush.

The van heads west on the South Ring, the rain now a
trickle, with the wipers back on medium and the noise
reduced.
'Where are you goin'?' the man asks, checking his mirror
as he changes lanes.
'I don't know. Anywhere. You can drop me wherever
you're going.'
'Are you in trouble?' The van picks up speed but then
slows as they reach the exit marked Bandon and the West.
The roads were darker and she could barely see him in the
gloom.
'Am I in trouble?' she asks. 'Are you in trouble so?'
'Cheeky. Here, I've a fresh pack of fags in the glove
compartment. Do you smoke?'
'Nah, I don't drink, neither. I used to but it didn't suit me,
so I stopped.'

She opens the glove compartment and an interior light lets her see the cigarettes, which she takes out and passes over. He slips them in the hold on his door.

'I'm Dessie, by the way.' He checks his mirror and goes for it, then takes the cigarettes and rips the plastic while leaning on the steering wheel, using deft fingers to flick the packet open. In seconds, he has one in his mouth but when he lights it with the electronic lighter from the dash, he overdoes the pressure and the top of the fag is smudged, much to his annoyance as he waves the extra smoke away.

'If you want to light fags on the move, you should practice more,' she tells him, catching him smiling as he flashes to the headlamps of an oncoming car.

He is quiet, concentrating on the road ahead, and she imagines the dark countryside around them. She knows it is vast and stretches for miles but it is blacked out and she can only guess so she switches to the line of hedgerows, playing games with the shadows.

'So where are you goin'?'

He douses his fag in the ashtray and returns his hand to the wheel, squinting against the glare when a car overtakes and burns its way ahead 'til it disappears.

'What's yer name?'

'Jael. It's short for Jaelyn.'

'Lovely name. Tell yah the honest, Jael, I've been on the road for a few days and I've been sleepin' in the back. I have an old mattress and a sleepin' bag. I don't want to scare you, love, but that's the truth. I will just pull over later and go to sleep but I can drop you in Bandon. There's a garage you can grab a burger and a sit-down coffee in. How about I drop you there?'

'So you live in this thing, Dessie, and you just drive about endlessly, heading nowhere?'

'I suppose. Only recently, though. I didn't always live like this. My life changed so I headed out on the road. I intend to keep goin' as long as I can pay for the diesel.'

Jael notices a sign for a place called Halfway. They pass a large roundabout, and then the road gets dark again.

'You must be goin' somewhere, Dessie. Everyone is goin' somewhere.'

'I am.' He laughs. 'I'm going to the same place as you!'

She smiles. 'Good one, Dessie.'

'So yer not scared then?'

'Scared of the night, not of you.'

'A man with a mattress in the rear of the van?' He's light-hearted so she isn't alarmed.

'Ah, you're not the type. I'll go for a burger with you. I'm starvin'. Is it far?'

'Ten, fifteen minutes.' He slaps his hands off the wheel and she can tell he's pleased.

The garage isn't busy and the food counter is nearly empty, though the remains of burnt food has a there-for-ages look. Dessie gets the last burger and Jael goes for a salad roll, and they both get coffee from the machine. He takes lots of milk but she doesn't use any. They take a stool by the window as the night closes in, with sporadic headlights out on the road. A girl is cleaning up the food area and throws away the remains of any food on display. A few minutes later and they might have got their order for nothing. Such a waste.

'I hate not smoking in these places. Used to love a fag and a coffee. I would smoke one before and after my burger.'

Dessie takes a bite but the burger is too big for his mouth so he bites off a tiny piece and puts it back down on his wrapping.

'Nah, the food is crap. You should bring it outside and smoke your fag.'

He looks at her like she has gone funny. 'It's raining again.'

'Yeah, find shelter. There's a fuckin' canopy, isn't there?'

'Yeah, I suppose, but we're here now.' He takes another bite, a little bigger than before.

They stay silent for a while, then Jael taps the counter. 'Don't let me forget my rucksack. It's the kinda thing I'd do – walk off without it.'

'Where will you stay the night?' He's drinking his coffee, looking away as the girl cleaning up comes to a table close by.

'I Dunno. I have money but I wanna keep it.' She waits for him to turn his attention back to her. 'Don't suppose I can have the front of the van?'

He looks at the remains of his burger bun, his expression making it obvious that he's not impressed. 'I suppose if I was a gentleman, you could sleep in the back – I'd take the front – but I'm not a gentleman so you can have the front. I'm not goin' to drag you away from civilisation so maybe we will pitch here for tonight. I have to see a fella later in a pub in the town. I can walk from here and you can stay in the van and listen to the radio.' He groans to himself before taking the last bite, washing it down with his coffee.

'Nah, I'll go with yah, you might get lost.'

He throws his eyes to heaven and smiles at her.

Dessie lights a fag, and they walk across a main road and down a few side streets. He's trying to protect his cigarette from the showers and drips from canopies guarding the shops. The pub is a small cubbyhole of a place at the front of a cheap hotel, a ten-minute walk from the garage. It's filthy, the bare floors full of dust, with discarded beer mats and crisp bags under the stools. The clientele are all men, except for a little old lady by the window, which is closed off with an array of dirty old memorabilia full of cobwebs. Jael smells the rain from the ten or so customers who, on a break from Covid restrictions, want to drink. Most of them are looking up, glued to a soccer match, with one or two shouting at the telly and raising their fists.

Dessie orders a pint and Jael has a spring water. The man he needs to see isn't there yet so, fumbling by a few ragged-looking men, they make their way into a corner to sit on a hardwood bench that looks stuck to the wall.

There is a goal in the match and two fellas near the bar jump from their seats and raise their fists at two other fellas at the far side. The old lady by the window stares ahead, oblivious to the goings on.

A man walks in, leading with a stick. His eyes are shut and he waves his stick as a kind of hello to all. Clearing the way with it, he walks close to the bar, feeling for stools that aren't there due to the Covid rules.

Dessie watches him for a while, then goes to move but changes his mind.

'Is that the man?' Jael asks.

'That's him, that's Blind Bill.'

'Why do yah need to see him?'

'These.' He holds out his hand to show her a gold ring and chain. The chain looks old but the ring newer, with a good-sized diamond that's sparkling.

'Stay here.' He gets up and makes his way towards Bill. Blind Bill is attracted to the noise on the telly, looking upwards, even though he can't see. His pint of stout slobbers down his chin and his overcoat and makes a brown pool on the floor. He nor anyone else seems to notice or, if they do, they pretend not to. The barman seems happy, too, like it's a regular occurrence.

Dessie speaks to the blind man, who turns towards him, his stick resting against his side. He puts his pint down on the bar and says something. Dessie holds his hand open and Jael sees the ring sparkle even in the low light.

Blind Bill drinks more from his pint, and it dribbles down his overcoat and onto the floor once again. Dessie doesn't say anything, just holds steady while Bill touches the jewellery. He picks up the ring first, then the chain, squeezing both like he's trying to calculate the combined weight. Then he hands Dessie back the ring but keeps hold of the chain. Dessie listens, then looks disappointed.

Back at the van, he prepares his bed, then opens the passenger door and gives Jael a blanket. He'd been quiet all the way back from the bar, like he was contemplating something serious.

'Here, I've a spare pillow. Rest yer head on my seat.'

'Thanks,' she says, 'I was gonna use my rucksack.'

'This will be better.' He throws the pillow to land on the driver's seat.

'How much did the blind man give yah for the chain?' she asks.

'Three hundred lousy quid.'

'Pittance.'

'Yeah, that was my mother's. Grandad always said it was very expensive.'

'What about the ring? It's beautiful.'

'He said it was worth nuthin'. The diamond is imitation. Told me I'd get better in a lucky bag.'

'Wow. Is he a jeweller?'

'Nah. He's a well-known thief. Lost his sight when some oul wan threw acid at him after he turned over her mother's house. He took everythin' the old woman had. She died soon after, her heart broken, as she had no insurance. It was a big story back then.' He looks up at the dark sky. 'I'm goin' to sleep, Jael, before it rains again and I get soaked standin' here.'

'Night, Dessie.'

He smiles and closes the door. Jael lies awake, wondering about the big cold world outside, and soon the rain starts again. She's just happy that the wipers don't need to go on, though they might have helped distract her from the past. No such luck.

Attracta was lying on the floor. Jael crossed the room three times, stepping over her, listening to make sure she was breathing. It was subdued and shallow, and every now and again she would grunt and sigh, she even farted once, and Jael was glad because, if she farted, she was alright, all her parts were in working order. She got a cushion from the two-seater sofa and placed it under her mother's head to soften her sleep. She rested quietly after that – no more grunts or farts. The offending gin bottle stood empty on the mantelpiece. It was innocuous in its own right, just an empty glass bottle with no attachment or responsibility to anyone. She heard a noise in the hall, then footsteps on the stairs, and froze. Peter Dunne. She didn't want him calling, and she didn't want him to see Attracta on the floor. He'd threatened her with eviction the last time and they needed him more now than ever.

The footsteps continued up the stairs and she sat on the two-seater, trying to figure things out. Peter had lost interest in Attracta but turned his attention to her. He started bringing her to pubs and clubs and plying her with drink. One night, she was so sick she conked out, and when she woke, he was standing over her, the length of his penis, big and bulbous, in his hand, jerking himself off and trying to push it into her mouth. She turned away and cried out and he went red in the face and said something she didn't quite hear. Then he stood up and pulled up his pants, and he started laughing like nothing had happened. She made her way to a chair, the worse for wear.

''Shh,' he'd said, 'you will wake Attracta and she will kill you. Look at the state of you.'

She'd stayed quiet, not wanting to antagonise him. He had such a temper, and his eyes were bulging with excitement.

3

Breakfast is good, and the hot-food counter is buzzing, brimming with delicious sausages, rashers, and eggs. Jael eyes the hash browns and Dessie orders an Americano, which the girl brings to him. He has a full Irish and Jael has two sausages and a hash brown. Dessie places his cigarettes and lighter on the counter and dumps his keys beside them.

'Where are you goin', Dessie? Go on now, tell me – I'm interested in you.' She doesn't look at him, she's too busy seeking out a toilet, which she'll need to visit soon.

'I'm going to County Mayo to see my sister, but first I'm driving everywhere and anywhere I've ever been, if you must know. I have to go see the blind man later, then the journey continues. I think I'll go out to Dunworley go walk the beach if the tide is low. Do you know it? Did you ever hear of it?'

'No, I didn't. I might head that way myself. I could do with a walk on the beach.'

He sips his Americano, taking it slow, eating bits of cut sausage in between. 'This is not like any other beach you ever seen. It's got these jagged petrol rocks, the sea rolls into little caverns in the cliffs.'

'Bring me, please.'

'I think yer stuck to me, Jael. Have you no place to go?'

'I'm at your service. The further away from the city for me, the better.'

'Are you going to finish that sausage?'

'Go on then.' She lifts it with her fork and drops it on his plate.

When they're done, she follows him as he walks fast over the bridge. The early shops are open and she's not sure whether to stop and go for a browse. She has money but not enough to buy big stuff, not that she's one for buying things, anyway, and she doesn't want to annoy him, either. He isn't waiting for her and turns right, down the narrow river path surrounded by bushes. Then he beckons for her to wait, so she does. She's taken by the dark river and the white surf as it breaks over the weir, where branches and plastic debris wash to the edge. Dessie sits on the first seat and lights a fag. He keeps looking down the path and checking his watch.

Jael sees the blind man, using his cane like an anteater seeks its prey. He walks at a slow pace, and once or twice he raises his cane in the air, maybe to see if it's raining or if the air is just moist from the river. With the bustling trucks and buses gone, the path is quiet and she hears the river's distinctive roar. Dessie speaks to Blind Bill and stubs his cigarette on the path. Bill reaches into the pocket of his overcoat and takes out a brown bag. He's speaking now as Dessie takes out banknotes from his jacket, the bundle wrapped in elastic. Blind Bill takes them and feels their weight, says something to Dessie, then walks back the way he came, waving his cane in the air as he goes. Dessie stares at the brown bag, opens it and checks its contents, then puts it into his jacket pocket. He lights another cigarette and stares at the river, like he knew it well but hadn't seen it for a long time.

The road to Timoleague is long and winding, with treacherous bends. At one point, as the van climbs, miles of rolling fields appear on Jael's left, while on the other side, she is looking over the Argideen valley, with the river meandering, almost reluctantly, to the sea.
'Did the blind man give you what you want?'
He didn't speak since Bandon, and she's trying to get him going.

'No.' He reaches for his cigarettes. 'He gave me what someone else wants. Took most of my cash along with the chain, and I gotta get to Mayo yet, and buy diesel, you know.'

He goes quiet, like he's only noticing the beautiful valley below, yet he can't enjoy it such are the twists and turns of the road, and soon, with the deep descent, he must concentrate.

'Wow, some road,' Jael says, but he's preoccupied and doesn't answer.

The van follows the bends down the steep hill to the bridge over the Argideen. She looks at the mud flats on the estuary and sees the magnificent ruins of the Franciscan Abbey, with its high walls and impressive tower. As they get closer, she spots old graves scattered within its walls. At least those who are laid to rest found safety and comfort in eternity. Instead of going over the bridge and along the estuary to Courtmacsherry, Dessie ploughs ahead along a nondescript road with sharp turns. They pass a meat factory and Jael thinks she hears screaming pigs. Then the road straightens and he picks up speed, still without saying a word.

He drives through a crossroads with signs left for Barryroe or straight for Dunworley. He slows to a stop and looks over the flooded fields where the sea has made furrows of swampland. Birds circle and scream over dead water, and on the other side, battered hedgerows protect harsh fields covered in weed. Dessie takes it all in and drives on 'til he sees the ocean and gasps in recognition. Then he turns left by the rear of an old farmhouse before swerving right along a track with moss growing at its centre. There is barely room for the van. He takes a quick right, then a sharp left before coming to a carpark overlooking Dunworley beach.

The ocean waves rattle, roar, and churn in the distance, like rolling cotton wool as they crash amongst the sturdy rocks below. Giant waves further out are repeating the churning and roiling until they explode on the shore and recede at speed.

Dessie gets out and starts taking photographs with his phone, going along the cliff to get shots at different angles. 'If we hurry, we might just beat the tide,' he says and takes off, with Jael prancing along behind him.

His footprints in the sand meander among the crop of rocks and, for a second, she thinks she's walking on Mars. He stands at the water's edge, taking photo after photo, and she figures he's just taking them for the sake of it. Less than twenty yards out, the sea is menacing as it vomits its frothy breath, the waves gathering and winding as if stuck on a spool.

'My sister Kathleen wants these.' He points at his phone, then turns and takes more shots of the cliffs, the waves on the sand getting louder and closer.

'She's dying, Jael. She has cancer, and possibly Covid. I told her I would revisit our favourite places, yah know, places we went as kids. Our grandad brought us around here. We stayed in a caravan in a little field just up the road. Yeah, this was one of the places he brought us.' His voice fades with the roar of the sea.

I apologise for sending you back to the places we shared as children, and you diligently obey my command, though it should have been a request. That was you, Dessie, as a kid, always obliging. It's how you stayed till the end. I have put you back there in every place of note that you and I visited as kids. I want you to update me on all – take photos – tell me what it's like to return. I have asked Jael to keep an eye on you, to watch you, she is to imagine our past. Together you can retrace our footsteps and relive our childhood journeys. Please, Dessie, bring me the proof that these places actually exist, that they are not just raw pieces of my imagination, stagnant and foul, rotting in my ageing mind. Bring me evidence of what is lost to us, please do.

Kate

Attracta was nursing her sore head and drinking gin from a mug because all the glasses had been broken. Peter stood by the window, looking out onto the Western road where the rain fell. The grass had a washed-and-rung-out look, and passing traffic lifted the stagnant water from the gullies up onto the pathways. Jael watched what he watched as she stood a foot behind him. He held the net curtain up high with his right hand.
'Richard asked for you expressly, Jael,' he said, 'and we wouldn't want to disappoint him now, would we? After all, he has made offers on three of my properties. Remember, girl, if Peter Dunne does well, you and her prosper.'
He let the curtain go and the room went dim, with only the Calor Gas fire providing light. Attracta was still wallowing in the gin. She leaned back in her armchair, tired from the effort.
'I hope you aren't leadin' my daughter astray, Peter Dunne. She is still a schoolgirl, you know. Not a very good one, mind, but a schoolgirl for all that!' She slurred her words in between cackles of laughter at her own joke.
'No trouble,' he said, his words edged with a nervous energy. 'Richard is a gentleman. He just likes pretty girls around his club. That's his business.'
'Yeah, girls is the operative word. I see he hasn't made any personal requests for me to drop by, after I cleaned his place and left his office spanking. He could eat his dinner off the floor.' She drank her gin down, then looked for more. The bottle contained another fill so she took her

time pouring it, leaving a drain so she'd have a tiny top-up for later.

'When we lived in Dublin, there was none of this, Peter,' she said. 'I was your muse then, wasn't I? You couldn't get enough of me when I stayed with Mrs Dunne. She doted on you, didn't she? Her sister's only child, and she told me how successful you were, and how the world was your oyster. And I believed her. Now you have no interest in me anymore. You have turned to my daughter, and she still a schoolgirl. Jesus, you will kill me yet.'

He took a seat opposite her so he could see how much gin was left in the bottle. 'The last time you came, you collapsed on Richard's floor. Don't you remember, Attracta? Jael here was mortified, with people stepping over you to get to the bar. The bouncers wanting to throw you out on the street. I was just about to let them but Richard insisted on bringing you to the back office. Don't you remember Jael patting your forehead with wet towels? Did you know she nursed you for an hour? Then Richard got his driver to bring you home, here yah are trying to undermine the man that feeds us. If he doesn't buy these properties, I will go under. Do you realise what that means, Attracta?'

She only took a sip this time. 'He's a funny one. His father is a foreigner – a bigshot. And he's always on the telly spouting on about this and that, with his leather skin, thinkin' he's God's gift. Richard Fanon, standin' for election. He's the type, alright, pays the minimum wage and makes his money from kids droppin' e-tabs and plyin' themselves with this stuff. It's the likes of him that make it, that's the way the world is now, Peter. He will make it – that's his future.'

Then she lifted her dress, revealing her thighs and underwear. 'Fed up with this, Peter? Are yah fed up with it? Like the younger version now?'

Quiet, Mam,' Jael said, breaking her silence. 'I only go and dance and have a few drinks, nuthin else. The driver brings us home, so we won't be that late. Isn't that true, Peter?'

'You're quiet,' Dessie says. He lights a fag, the van sitting in a small layby. Jael looks at the view. Across the moorland and the sweeping hills, she imagines a lake of blue lies in secret within the saucer-shaped valley.

'Yah see up there, the tunnel they blasted through the mountain?'

'I do,' she answers, distracted by the wild sheep painted in blues and pinks. They're shaggy – a hardy type – and some have vicious-looking horns.

'When we come out the other side, we'll be in Kerry.'

'Really? I've never been to Kerry. That's a first.'

He smokes his cigarette to a stump, crushes it in his ashtray, then slides down the window, the cloud of smoke swirling as fresh air wafts in. 'I need to take more photos in Kerry for Kathleen, you know.'

'Great.'

'She was good to me. Like, growin' up, there was just us. Our parents died and our grandad brought us up, you know, which was hard for him, and it was hard for us as well but he did his best, mind, in the way of the times. You probably don't get me.' He lights another fag, smoking it out the window.

Jael sees herself in the side mirror and tries to fix her fringe but the sheep distract her once again as they trot up the road. She worries for them as a car approaches but they just hop to the side at the last moment and reach the safety of the ditch.

The tunnel is hewn through the mountain. It isn't long and she can see the bright light on the other side. Dessie keeps the van steady in the middle, away from the water flowing down the sides, the rock uneven but solid. Without warning, they're surrounded by light as the vast valley below appears and she can see for miles. The van swerves left to stick to the narrow mountain road, sending sheep scattering over a small wall. They have odd colours, too. Dessie smiles as they drive through a stone arch, the road winding for miles ahead, descending all the time. It gave her the opportunity to remember things she'd rather forget.

Richard Fanon was thirty-two. Peter moaned about it regularly. How could a fella of thirty-two outdo an entrepreneur like himself who was tipping forty? But he never let on to Richard. No, he was all over him. He brought her through the club. It was a Thursday night and quiet as regards people but the music still rocked. She couldn't hear Peter properly so she just followed him into the back room where Richard had his office. Richard greeted them with his customary shrug, like that was the precursor to his real self. He smiled. It was spontaneous, almost combustive. She guessed that he smiled like that since he was a toddler, and she pictured him playing with toy bricks with the same expression on his face.
'Dunner,' he exclaimed, looking at the money he was counting on his desk. 'Takings are shite, I may have to reconsider my offers, or maybe I can afford to buy only one of your houses, huh?'
Peter didn't get the joke and was about to protest when Richard added, 'Don't get yer knickers in a twist, I'm jokin' yah!'
Jael couldn't get used to this man of Libyan descent speaking with a neutral Irish accent. It just didn't fit his tanned face or his overall demeanour.
'You're lookin' well, Jael. Love the dress.'
It was tight on her. Peter paid for it but she got to pick it, much to Attracta's chagrin.
'Fuckin' Thursday's useless,' Richard lamented. 'Roll on Saturday and we will be turnin' them away. Last Saturday

was mad.' He stopped counting the money and looked at Peter. 'Will you go and check if it's all going well, Peter? Go have a drink. I want to chat with Jael for a few minutes.' He remained light-hearted but something within his voice betrayed a seriousness. Peter looked at her for a second, then left.

'How do you do it when you have school tomorrow?' Richard stood up and went to his own mini bar by the window.

Jael could see the traffic pass on the street but he pulled the drape, then all she saw were shadows. He poured himself a whiskey, then one for her, and brought it to her. Her tummy fluttered as she stood in the middle of the room but she clinked his glass out of politeness.

'Come, we can sit on the sofa for a few minutes. It will be more comfortable. You have such a beautiful figure, Jael, you really are a beauty.'

She sat beside him, her dress exposing her thighs, which she tried to correct by crossing her legs.

He pulled her crossed leg back. 'Don't do that. Let me see you – I want to see you.'

She tried to make light chat. 'I won't be going to school in the morning, Richard. I'll be too tired, yah know!'

'Oh, yes, I understand.' He kissed her on the lips.

She didn't mind, as she found him attractive, and his kiss was gentle. His tongue explored hers and his left hand rubbed her thigh as he moaned and made muffled sounds deep within him.

'You are a good girl, Jael.' He stood over her – a car door banged out on the street – and he loosened his belt and his trousers dropped to cover his shoes.

He dropped his underpants then. His penis was big and strong, with dark patchy skin. He moved closer and beckoned her to take it in her hand. She did as he wanted because she wanted to please him. His eyes were wild as

he stared down at her and she sensed a meanness about him that wasn't there before.
'You have to do this for me. Be a good girl now.'

4

Elizabeth Cullen was a mad child who was into things. She moved about the estate like a minesweeper, busy foraging under hedges. The girl was a great collector, and everything had a value. In winter, she went door to door swapping comics. She had a mantra she used when checking your swaps: "Have, haven't, don't want." I could hear her in Mrs Stubbs, the shrill sound of her voice echoing from the dividing porch: "Have, haven't, don't want." – the 'don't want' said with derision. Elizabeth was fierce good-looking, though, her skin tender, her face adorned with high cheekbones and a string of curls that reached her chin. She had dark, haunting eyes that withdrew all approval 'til you were in. If and when you were in, she reserved a beaming smile for you.

Her family were one of the better off ones on the block. It was just Elizabeth and her need to do what she enjoyed. She was always busy in summer, catching bees in a jar and charging a penny for a Teddy Back and tuppence for a big Black Bumbler. The street kids were suckered in and Dessie was a prime candidate. The delighted children ran home with their jam-jar lids closed tight. The idea was to pierce a hole in the lid so the bees had air but the black bumblers and the Teddy Backs invariably went to the bottom of the jar and began to fade. Dessie found out that putting the hedging in with the bees didn't help, as one by one the bees faded and became still. Sometimes they died quietly but other times they gave one almighty buzz before passing away. Grandad warned him but he wasn't the listening type. He cried sitting on the chair beside the black & white television. Grandad wanted to throttle Liz Cullen and her whole family for causing the upset. I defended her, pointing out, much to Dessie's disgust, that he should have known the bees would die through experience. Like, when did they ever not die? They always died. Every year we went through the same process. Grandad didn't want to hear my logic or views on the matter and told me to go to my bedroom while he sat with Dessie in an effort to distract him from his melancholy. I was glad with the quiet of my room; the window to the world was enticing. There she was, Liz Cullen, still selling her wares to the unsuspecting kids. The Black Bumblers were making mighty efforts to escape, which seemed to excite the kids even more and entice them to part with their coppers. Johnny Byrne appointed himself Liz's aid. He was in charge of handing over the jars once the coins had changed hands. Johnny was a big fan of Elizabeth's, even though he was two years older. He smiled a lot, like really a lot. Somehow, he'd got smacked on the back at the stroke of midnight in the midst of a big smile and was cursed ever after. And it wasn't even just a smile of sudden amusement but one of everlasting derision, which made him look like he was being smart even when he wasn't.

Liz looked up, seeing my head pressed against the window. She smiled and held a jar full of black bumblers in victory. It was like she'd won them in a battle. I smiled back. I wanted to keep in with her. Of all the kids in our street, she was the one who was going to be something. I was always going to keep in with her, even if it meant swallowing my pride on occasion.

I went to the toilet and I knew Grandad and Dessie were watching an old western by the shooting and bullets ricocheting off stuff. I was glad they were both peaceful and quiet and the house had returned to normal. I found out later that Grandad had made Dessie promise not to indulge in bees again and to watch his cash. He made him empty his jar in the flower garden out the back. Dessie did as he was told and shut up about the tragedy.

I was glad that Grandad never got a hold of Liz Cullen, partly because he forgot about the whole thing the next day, and partly because he liked Mr and Mrs Cullen and thought them respectable. He wouldn't have wanted to embarrass himself or Dessie. Also, he wouldn't know what Liz Cullen looked like and, if she called to the door for me, he would get all flustered and call me from the bottom of the stairs, telling me my friend was at the door. He never said 'Liz' because he wasn't sure who she was, even though he knew that she was one of the neighbours. Liz didn't think anything of it. She always referred to him as 'your beautiful grandad', or 'your old grandad'. She obviously held him in affection, as someone she saw come and go daily.

Of course, Grandad still had a reputation amongst some of the elderly. He was seen as a gentleman when he worked on the buses but people still thought him odd for that, which is hard to take. He was regarded as a kind man and a kind bus conductor, if a bit over the top. He helped folk on and off the buses and waited for people who were dashing to catch the bus at the designated stop, even if he was running late. It stood to him, even if most of these people thought him to have gone mad in later life. Sure, that's their business, I guess.

A few years later, Liz called one blistering sunny day and we headed off to the baths in Dun Laoghaire. I was delighted but the only problem was that Johnny Byrne tagged along. Lately, he'd stuck to her like a sticking plaster – there was no getting rid of him but, somehow, Liz didn't seem to mind or care. She lazed on the back seat of the bus upstairs, and Johnny paid both their fares, while I had to pay my own. I had saved my pocket money that Grandad gave me for doing chores around the house. We walked down through the people's park. It was splendid, the lawns lush, with pretty red and yellow flowers in private beds beyond the park benches where old folk congregated. Children ran by to get to the playground and its swings and monkey puzzles that took up one corner. We stopped by a fountain, where the water had turned a green stagnant colour, such was the heat. Liz lay on her cardigan, exhausted by the sun. Johnny rested his back against the fountain's concrete surround. I stood for a minute, listening to the train passing under the promenade as it entered the tunnel to Dun Laoghaire station.

Neither Johnny nor Liz spoke, so I said, "We'd better not delay or the pool will be packed. I wanna get my body wet and cool down, the heat is murder."

Liz lifted her head like she'd just remembered that I was in her company. "Plenty of time for that, Kate, I'm bunched. And I love the sun on my face. Johnny will go on with you if you need to go."

"Nah," I said, "I'll wait for you – no fun without yah."

She got to her feet without enthusiasm. The heat of the sun made her hair curl even more. She was bronzed, not burnt like me and Johnny. We crossed the road by the rail track that disappeared under the promenade.

"I wanna ice-pop," she stated. "I'm parched, and I can't swim if I'm parched."

Johnny bought two ice-pops in the little shop inside the door. I looked on as they licked and sucked them 'til the tops got narrow. I had my togs under my clothes so I undressed by the side of the five-foot and basked in the sun, knowing that soon I would enter the glistening water and bravely duck under to feel the cold water encase my body like a block of ice.

While Johnny finished his ice-pop first, Liz continued licking hers with a fast use of her tongue. I looked on, envious. The orange and green goo dropped onto her thigh and she wiped it with her towel. The older crowd were out on the Jetty for a swim in the open sea. They swam out about a mile and were all strong, robust swimmers, unlike me, who couldn't swim a stroke despite Grandad getting on to me about it and offering to pay for lessons.

"Are yahs getting in?" Liz asked, like she was sad to have finished her ice-pop and was still parched. Her voice sounded hoarse and throaty. Johnny Byrne did what he always did – he gave that dreadful smile, then slipped off his T-shirt and got in, lowering his body from the side. I watched him from the bench. He was shivering, and he looked like he was about to abandon all but then he dived under, and a few seconds later he appeared under the slide in the five-foot.

"Come on in, it's gorgeous." He is moving fast to avoid a fat kid who came barrelling down the slide and made an enormous splash.

I eased myself in to about three feet of water and rested my elbow on the side. Liz jumped in and swam to Johnny, who was taking refuge beyond the slide, and chatted to him while treading water. The sun glistened, and the action of bodies created small ripples that danced to the edge, causing an overflow. All of a sudden, I was aware of the noise – the constant roar of screaming kids, the voluminous belly flops, the shivering shy ones who stayed out of the water but stood at the edge.

"Are you getting down?" Liz said.

She was out of the water, standing over me. For a second, her towel blocked the sun.

"I'm alright, this is what I do. I might kneel down in a few minutes and duck my face in." I wanted to sound brave but she knew me and knew when I was lying.

"It's easy. Put your face in the water and do this with yer arms." She showed me the action. "Go on." She moved a foot and the sun ripped into me again and my skin was burning.

"Go on, try it. I'm here if you need me."

"Alright," I said, frustrated with myself and not wanting to fail her challenge, so I did her actions, heading for the shallow end, knowing that if it didn't work, my knees would touch the bottom.

"See." She smiled. "Yah can do it, Kate."

She was right. I swam a yard, then swam another one and a bit. I swam right by the edge of the five-foot, so if I got tired, I could grab on but I didn't need to, I was fine. Liz and Johnny went to the Big Tank and left me. I couldn't get enough. Sometimes, I stood up and waited, sensing people were noticing me and my great swimming process, and I wondered what Dessie and Grandad would say if they saw me. I could picture Dessie's disbelieving face as he doubted my story.

Liz bought me an ice-pop on the way out. Johnny had to go and meet his mother in the Elphin hotel where she worked, so Liz and I took a stroll down towards Sandycove. It was still a lovely evening but the sun had died a little, leaving behind a pleasant breeze. The sea took on a dark-blue colour and swished about like it was enjoying itself.

We stood leaning on the railings at Bug Rock. The sound of the kids in the baths had dissipated, and only a few adults swam, with most of them in the big tank or in the open sea.

"Do you think I could swim to Holyhead?" Liz wanted to know.

"Yeah, you might. I wouldn't make that rock out there."

We both laughed at the ridiculousness of my comment and the sad way that I announced it and announce was the right word.

"I'd float most of the way," Liz said, "to save energy. Floating saves lots of energy, like a plane gliding saves fuel."

"Does it?" I asked, all genuine. "Come on, Liz, let's go down to Sandycove. But I won't tell my grandad – he's always going on about those dirty oul lads prancing around in their nude. 'Dirty fuckers', he calls them, 'Showin' off their tackle to the world'." Liz wanted to ask me something, but I was on a roll. "Like we want to see their big hairy mickies. They're all paedophiles, that's what me grandad says, an' he's right, Liz."

She stayed quiet, like the conversation was beyond her, or sickened her to the stomach more like but, whatever, she didn't say nuthin for a fair bit. As we walked down the promenade, getting further from the town, the crowds coming towards us started to thin out.

People were getting ready to leave Sandycove, with the best of the day done. Young men walked towards the Forty Foot, carrying fishing rods, some of them with their girlfriends in tow. They looked healthy and chirpy as they bantered amongst themselves. A few posh boys pulled over, with Kayaks on the roof of their station wagon. Liz smiled at them. I admit, they were tasty, good-looking fellas, with blonde complexions. They looked well-nourished and athletic they didn't possess the vulgar innocence of the fishermen.

One of the boys took an interest in Liz, though he was much older, like, I'd say he was eighteen. In fairness, it didn't last long – he might have just been flirting. He told her she had a golden complexion and a great body. When he and his companion put the Kayaks in the water, he smiled up at us and, as they took off, shouted, "You're a ride, young one," in a fake accent well below his station. Liz laughed and wasn't at all offended. She ran to the end of the sea rocks to wave at her suitor.

I wanted to go for a walk around by Joyce's Tower. After such a warm day, it was getting cooler. The sea was growing white horses near where we sat, and the wind was in our face so we set off and passed the Forty Foot, which was strangely quiet. Fisherman were sitting on the rocks, fixing their tackle. That's what put me off fishing – all that messing about with tackle, spending hours doing and undoing knots, and trying to save weights and hooks that were stuck in seaweed and under rocks.

We met this dapper fellow outside Joyce's Tower. He was one of those Irishmen who have affected a British accent for some reason. This man wore a white suit, was clean shaven, and very tall. He wore a wide-brimmed hat that threatened to leave his head any second with the breeze.

"Would you mind very much if I asked you to take a photograph? I want to get one of me standing with the tower in the background. I'll probably frame it, though my sister frames things for me and she is being rather difficult right now." He handed his expensive camera to Liz, who sized him up. I looked on without much interest.

"Oh," he said, his voice soft, "try not to shake, as it distorts everything. If you could keep your hands as steady as possible."

Liz smiled and nodded but she gave me a rather cheeky grin before she clicked.

"Take another, please," he said, and this time he took off his hat.

"Ready?" Liz said and clicked once again. She walked forward and handed him the camera. As he took it, I noticed that he had delicate hands that had never seen manual work.

"You girls live near here?"

I went to speak but Liz beat me to it.

"No, we live about four miles away."

"Oh." He examined his camera for Liz's paw marks but, satisfied, hung it around his neck, supported by its thick strap. "I have a flat around the corner. I used to live with my sister on Corrig avenue but…I did tell you about her. If you would like to come visit sometime, let me know and I could show you my photographs and make you lemonade."

Unused to being invited anywhere, Liz said, "That would be lovely."

I didn't say anything. At the same time, I was curious as to what his flat was like. Was it clean and tidy or a mess? Did he have scraps of uneaten food everywhere in his kitchen? Judging by the way he dressed, it was most likely very clean and tidy.

"Maybe tomorrow or the next day? I will walk with you if you are going my way and I can show you where it is?"

"Sure," Liz said, her tone respectful, "we are going this way."

"Excellent," he said, and we walked around by the Forty Foot to Sandycove and turned right at the corner heading back towards Dun Laoghaire. He stopped just as we reached the promenade. "That's my place. I live in number seven. It's upstairs at the very top." And off he went across the road.

I saw the kayaks returning in the last of the sunlight. In the distance, the mail boat was coming, blocking the view across the sea to Howth.

"Well, well," Liz announced, waving at the lads in the Kayaks. They didn't wave back. "We gotta get him a name, Kate. How about Mister Dazzle?"

"He's some dazzler, Liz, and I'm tellin' yah, I won't be drinkin' any lemonade or lookin' at photos up there."

We looked up at the top window of his house. I thought I saw him standing in the shadow, but Liz said she could see nuthin'.

5

Dessie goes through Kenmare. The roads are better if still winding.

'You need a loo?' he asks as Jael moves her legs about trying to find comfort. 'Put them up on the dash if it makes you feel better.' He's smoking again. 'Are you hungry?' he asks through a cloud of smoke. 'Will we stop for a coffee?'

'If you want. I'm not hungry but a coffee sounds good. A girl can always use a toilet.'

Dessie gives her a hard look, then turns back to the road. The bends come at him thick and fast as he heads towards Sneem.

'When I was a kid, I knew this fella called Murt – he was a heavyset fella but not fat, like, he was very athletic and popular amongst all the fellas that hung out together. His only problem was he could never make up his mind. He was ridiculous. The boys would call for him on a Sunday to go to the flicks, and he wouldn't be ready. They'd get really pissed with him because they wanted to see the B movie. If they were late, they had to walk in right in the middle of it, and if they couldn't catch up with the storyline, they gave Murt a right ribbing. He wouldn't commit to it. Sometimes he'd go get ready and come with us, and other times he'd just sit at his kitchen table drinking tea, with all the boys surrounding him, waiting on him to move, but he might not bother his hole. Are you like that, Jael? Are you like Murt?'

'Hah, Dessie, what makes you think that about me?'

'Dunno, you're slow to answer questions. I know you have some reason to be on this road with me but you won't tell me, and I doubt if you will ever tell me. When I wanna stop for food, you can't be arsed. It's like you want me to keep drivin' forever, like, whatever it is you're running away from is chasing you, if you stop, it might just catch up with you!'

'I'm not afraid, Dessie, and there isn't anyone chasin' me. I'm not like your friend Murt, I'm not like him at all. I'm just amazed that you fellas were still stupid enough to call for him. Like, how many B pictures did you miss?'

'You don't get it, Jael, it wouldn't have been the same without him, and he knew that.'

He stops at a roadside cafe outside Sneem. Jael sees the sun disappear, dragged over the horizon by a cloud. The ocean is stirred.

The coffee is good but the fare is limited, as this place is really an antiques-and-souvenir establishment. The lady serving is super friendly and efficient. She isn't busy so has time to chat, used to a good hustle.

'Are ye on holidays?' she asks, sizing them up.

They are sitting outdoors so Dessie lights up, then butters his scone.

'The business is terrible since the Covid. Most years we'd be flat out.' All the while she talks, she cleans the only other outdoor table. She is vigorous, and it doesn't bother her that she hasn't received a response.

'No, we're not on holiday,' Jael tells her. 'Just passing through. '

'Where are you heading?' She stands by their table, awaiting an answer.

'Mayo,' Jael says.

Dessie takes a puff, then a bite of his scone. The woman looks at him like she's wondering why a man of his age is alone with a beautiful young girl who doesn't seem to be his daughter.

'My sister lives there. She's not well so we are going to see her.' It's clear that he feels he has told her enough.

'Is this yer daughter?' she asks, as blunt as can be.

'No, I'm not.' Jael laughs. 'I just want to visit Mayo – I've never been there before.'

Not satisfied at all, the woman leaves and goes inside her shop, where she makes a lot of noise as she pretends to sort out her wares.

Dessie smiles at Jael and they get up and leave.

He turns off the main road at Caherdaniel. They barely fit down the narrow lane, which has overgrown trees and bushes on both sides, scraping against the van. All of a sudden, it all opens up and there's a big empty carpark.

'More post-Covid phenomena,' Dessie says, repeating it like he's a parrot. 'I just don't get this Covid thing.'

Jael knows to stay quiet. She's looking at the view and the mighty ocean crashing to the golden sand. He is out of the van, lighting up, and he walks ahead of her onto the deserted beach. This is unlike Dunworley. There are no magnificent rocks, only a series of small coves and stranded islands, and the remains of a volleyball court carved into the sand. He starts taking photos, clicking here and there, then walks right up to the water's edge and clicks just as a giant wave releases its froth.

'This is Kates's favourite place – or one of…'

You have found Derrynane. Jael is watching you, in case you leave anything out in your report. Oh, how I love our time there with you and Grandad, the games we played. I remember the ice-cold water spraying froth over your head, as Grandad lifted you above his shoulders and dropped you unceremoniously, headfirst. I watched you gurgle and gasp as you returned to the air. I hugged you but you pushed me away because I was so cold, then we laughed eating Grandad's picnic. Coke and crisps. He managed to give us an apple each and then told us we couldn't swim for at least forty-five minutes. It didn't matter that we had double pneumonia sharing the one and only small towel he brought. I remember you laughing, looking like a fish with the wet sand caked on your face.

Kate

Jael loses him there as the wind whips up hard, their
clothes sticking to their bodies, with tiny air bubbles
forming to protect her skin. He turns away from her to face
the ocean, mouthing words like he's having a conversation
with someone. She wonders is he talking to ghosts. He
takes a deep breath, goes to leave, then turns back towards
the van. She sits on the sand and waits for him to end his
ritual.
'Fuck it,' he says, turning back to face the ocean and
starting to strip. She watches him throw his jumper and T-
shirt onto the sand. Then he drops his pants and underpants
and stands before her, naked, though he doesn't look at
her, he just keeps staring at the ocean. Then, as quick, he is
gone, crashing into the waves. He disappears for a few
seconds before resurfacing. Jael can barely see his head.
She thinks to herself that he has a funny body, his belly
like a basketball, his chest hairy with tufts growing from
his nipples, his back slender, like his bottom, but his legs
are hairy. He is an ape but not one bit sexual or nasty. He
is just an aging man.
His head bobbles like a beach ball, disappearing amidst the
large waves. As they crash, she expects to see pieces of
him but she only spies his bald head, with hair stuck to its
sides as he swims outwards. She's afraid for him, and he
stops and turns and does an exaggerated overarm, like he's
in an Olympic race and he must win the gold medal. She
watches him float, his eyes scanning the cloudy sky like
he's searching for something. He doesn't flinch for what
seems like minutes on end – his stare catatonic.
'Are you alright, Dessie? Will I go to the van and get you
a towel?'
He doesn't move, continuing to float and stare at the sky.
The sun breaks through. Just a little at first, then it lights

the ocean beyond him in a straight line that hits him like a jerking bolt of lightning. He sighs and turns, then swims back to the shore. This time Jael sees his tiny, shrivelled penis, and his crop of pubic hair that guards it. She knows she's staring but is really fascinated with his oversized stomach. It is huge, and his clothes hide it well.

'Will I go get you a towel?'

'Yes, do, thank you,' he says, the tears flowing down both cheeks.

She runs back towards the van while he stays put, the water dripping from him onto the dry sand.

He brings her on through Waterville, and she likes the quaint main street, the roads that are tight and surrounded by soft grasses, and a magnificent golf course by the shoreline. Beyond it, he turns left down a country road with deep ditches and desolate fields. They pass an old village and an old hotel, and he pulls into a carpark facing a beach which has a large island just offshore that has a ruin, and the tide is low so they can walk out to it.

Dessie farts, loud and long, and doesn't apologise. Jael is overcome and jumps out while he lights a fag, waving his lighter around to kill the smell.

The air outside is clear and fresh as it fills her senses, and the waves are hitting the shore, soft and with far more respect than at Derrynane.

Attracta leaned over Jael, her swimsuit wet through. Jael had been warm but now shivered and complained to her mother.

'What's with your nonsense, Jael? I was reaching for my fags. Would you have me go without?'

'No,' Jael snapped, 'but yer drownin' me.'

Attracta laughed, showing her gammy green front tooth. Jael put it down to all the wine and spirits but Attracta blamed 'Old Thomas', the dentist her mother sent her to as a child. "He made a bollicks of the fillin's. It's true, I had to go to the dental hospital. Yer man there nearly choked me with one of his tubes. I wriggled for my life when I was gargling the fuckin' thing."

Peter came back with the coffee, and Jael was glad of it, as the sun had gone, the clouds conspiring to make it cold. The sea at Garretstown sulked, then changed colour.

'Coffee – reminds me of sobriety and what that was like.' Attracta laughed at what she thought was a joke.

'Plenty of sugar in yours,' Peter said, almost at a shout. Jael remained quiet. Let them at it.

'I don't need sugar, Peter, you know I'm sweet.'

Jael looked at her mother. The alcohol hadn't destroyed her body yet. She was taut, with wide hips, and still had a decent, pert bottom, though her main attributes were her hair and face. She had strong, piercing eyes, and with makeup she was stunning. Peter still liked her. Jael could tell. It was like he washed away all the drunken memories and painted himself a new reality without them.

He put his hand on her right shoulder as he sat beside her on the sand. 'We will head soon.' He kicked the sand with his bare foot. 'The best of the day is gone.'

Jael picked up her spare towel and placed it over her legs, then made a space in the one she was sitting on. Peter looked away, interested as some fella's tried to launch a boat against the increasingly large waves.

Attracta was smoking again. She inhaled deep and exhaled it away towards the sea wall, then up to the sky.

'I'm getting dressed,' Jael announced. Peter looked at her like she was losing it.

Attracta got to her feet and fetched her robe from a supermarket carrier bag. 'I'm going to wear this home. No point in getting dressed before a nice shower.'

Peter smiled at Jael, who kept her second towel around her as she dressed. She was going to turn her back on him

*but then decided to stare at him to make him uneasy, what
with his beady eyes looking her up and down.*
*When home, he brought Attracta upstairs to his flat to
shower and dress – the excuse being his shower had a
stronger flow as it was electric. Jael heard her laugh, then
scream playfully, then laugh again. All went quiet and she
didn't come down again 'til nearly nine and only ate half
of the supper Jael had made for her.*
'Not hungry, mother?'
*'Not really, it's been a long day. I'd love a drink but I
haven't the money.'*
'Didn't he have anything?'
*'Nah, he wasn't in a generous mood. Evidently, I don't
please him like I used to.'*
*'Oh.' Jael looked out through the kitchen window to the
last of the light. It made the flowerbeds dark, the shadows
menacing.*

Dessie drives up these narrow boreens that lead to a
winding road with a wall separating small fields that soon
become cliffs. The road is narrow in parts and they have to
stop and reverse to allow cars and a tractor pass. He is
sweating and could do with a shower or a bath. Jael goes
to tell him, feeling she knows him well enough, but he's
concentrating on the dangerous road, so she leaves it. The
road opens a little and she sees small fields with makeshift
divides, with a few cattle roaming like they are wild. All
the while, the van climbs until it stops without warning.
Dessie pulls it onto the grass siding to allow other traffic
pass.
'That's it,' he says, pointing to a ruin at the top of the
headland. 'Come on.'
She gets out and feels the cool breeze so reaches for her
jumper, which warms her a little. Dessie is halfway across
a narrow field, then climbs over a flimsy wire fence, and
she goes to race after him but pulls up and decides to take

her time. She still feels the coolness of the breeze. The breeze becomes wind as she climbs, and it carries the scent of wildflowers. She gasps at the view – miles of ocean, with rolling mountains towering over majestic but empty sandy beaches.

Ahead, Dessie's out of shape, his body trundling on as he gets nearer the ruin. He still moves fast, though, with determination. Here and there, he pulls out his phone and takes photographs. As she reaches the top, she sees why he is so eager. Beyond the sprawling ocean is lit by the magnificent glisten of the evening sun, and there before her, just like she could touch them, are Skellig Michael and the elephant-shaped smaller rock, and she imagines seabirds flocking around them in a frenzy. In the distance, she spies a small boat, like a tiny dot stuck to the map of the world. Dessie goes inside the ruin and she waits for him, forced to take a deep breath against the power of the wind. The cliff edge is guarded by a crumpled wall, with loose stones everywhere. He comes out and they move to a nearby, more modern construction.

On Bolus head. When we went there, Grandad riddled all those kids with his single automatic pipe. Such a shame he has left us. I wore a white frock that blew up by my hips when I ran. That grass was full of sheep dung, and I was jumping and skipping along. Thinking back, how did he wear a suit up there? It must have been so uncomfortable, but he did. A gale blew but it was a gorgeous day – it was just a windy spot, with Grandad taking refuge to light his pipe and the sweet smell in the air as the wind spread the aroma. The kids loved him, and he loved shooting them. Watching them roll down the hill, tumble, tumble, down.

Kate

'This is Bolus head,' he says, 'and that was once a weather station. We were here one summer many years ago. Kathleen and me, and all of these kids who were running wild – think they were from an orphanage or something. Anyhow, Grandad kept shooting them with his pipe, and they were dying in all sorts of mocking ways, tumbling down the hill, holding their heads. The kids really took to him. Kate and I used to say that "he shot 'em dead on Bolus Head".

Jael laughed as he lit a fag. It wasn't the best place to light up – he had to go right into a corner to beat the wind to get a flame.

'This was an old lookout. They'd be watching for French or Spanish ships. A good spot, too, as you can see.' He takes more photos, both interior and exterior. Then they walk back downhill towards the van. 'I think we'll park in the beach carpark overnight. They have a toilet there so at least we have that.'

He is quiet all the way back down the mountain. Jael takes the time to scan the views over Waterville, the breakers sailing to it in a continuous torrent. The hills leading to the mountains remind her of freedom, refreshing her enthusiasm. She glances at Dessie, who is watching the narrow road so intensely she feels for him. His loss is palpable, and his determination to entertain his sister with these photographs is heroic.

They are back on proper roads, surrounded by ditches and swirling montbretia, with a torrent of water running along deep channels on either side. He drives into the empty car park and Jael spots some fellas pitching a tent on the beach, deep in discussion as the sea rolls in behind them.

'Do you wanna go first?' Dessie says, reaching for his fags.

'Ok.' She gets out and starts walking.

6

Dessie drives slowly. As they pass a fairy fort, Jael is captivated, never having seen one before. She wants to ask him to stop but his focus on the road is intense, with sweat dripping from his forehead. His skin is boiling underneath his T-shirt, and she reckons he really needs a shower as it's the same one he wore yesterday, and the day before. She will start looking for a laundry the next big town they hit. There wasn't any in Cahersiveen. Well, maybe there was but she didn't see it. She wonders does he realise that he's starting to smell. At least the odour is confined for now to his sweat and not his farts.

He drives to a place called Coonanna Pier, where they are greeted by a few roaming hens and a small pier guarding modest boats.

'When we visited here with Grandad, it lashed. I never seen rain like it – belted off the sea. We had to stay in the campervan, cleanin' the windows with the back of our hands to see out.'

Jael was ahead of him, taken with the perfect stillness of the water. It was like an ice rink – so cold and solid looking, with screeching seabirds all round her. The hills opposite where really giant drumlins growing from the seabed, and wild smells came to her where the wildflowers had mixed with the sea air.

Dessie catches up, now at ease, smiling as they come to a rail at the pier's end. 'He had to bring us back to Cahersiveen. They had a Wimpy back then, and Kate and me stuffed our faces with burgers. Thinkin' back, it was very modern of my grandad to go to a place like that. He was a contrary oul bugger but he tried.'

Jael smiles, not fully getting him. *What's so modern about getting a burger?*

'Three Latvian men were drowned here a few years back,' he says as they retrace their steps and head back to the hens. He's busy taking photos of the small boats, the still water, and the mounds of earth that shadow all. 'Imagine, going fishing – a day out with yer mates – and none of you come back. What is it, Jael, just another statistic? The only ones that remember them are their loved ones. Their families. It's all about blood. The masses move on. Place these things on the back burner and folk forget the following day that a tragedy happened. Way of the world, Jael.' He keeps clicking, and Jael is afraid his phone might explode.

I was so alone that day we stopped at Coonanna Pier. I think it was the first time that I really missed Mother. I started bleeding. That wasn't the kind of thing that I could talk to Grandad or you about. I was glad it was raining, and we got stuck inside. I didn't want to risk walking down that pier. When we went to the Wimpy, I sat near the wall so I couldn't be seen. It was the first time that I had a premonition. I saw my life unfold before me. Wondering at first how we managed to lose both our parents at once. In truth, I hardly knew them at all. It was a mother I missed that day, not my mother as such. My whole life opened up with a bite of a burger. Everything until death.

Kate

The journey back to Cahersiveen is better, as the fresh air at the pier has dried out his sweat. When he lights a fag, it is almost a blessing, the smoke eradicating all the older smells. They pass the fairy fort again but this time she's content to look on from the road.
She's tired and rests her eyes but jolts when he comes to a screaming halt and pulls into a layby where she sees a sign for Kells Bay but nothing from the map, he showed her earlier. This bronzed boy of about fourteen stares at the

van, a bundle of possessions under his arm. Dessie urges
her to move and make room, and the boy climbs in and
takes the middle seat.

'My name is Aswar,' he says, his voice soft, like he is
announcing his limits as regards the use of English.

'Where are you going?' Dessie asks, pronouncing every
word fully.

'I go to Tralee… I go to Killarney and I meet family.'
Aswar is pleased with himself.

'Where do you live?' Jael asks out of politeness.

'I live where der is a hunger – very bad.'

'A hunger strike.' Dessie is pleased with his intelligent-
sounding response.

'Hunger strike – all the people hate it in Cahersiveen. It is
no good – so der is a hunger strike.'

Dessie is driving again.

'The Star… Yes, that is it, it is called the Star.'

'Chicken coup,' Dessie says under his breath, but loud
enough for Jael to hear it.

Aswar smiles like he gets it. Jael puts her feet up on the
dash, not altogether sure that she likes the extra legs in the
cab.

Then Dessie skids to halt, catching both Aswar and Jael by
surprise.

'Do you have the Covid, son?'

Aswar, putting it all together, smiles. 'Nah, sir, my muther,
she had the Covid but she is much better this month, but de
people have it in the Star. Dats why my muther make me
go. She says, "Aswar, you go see your uncles and your
cousins in Killarney." We don't know where dey are but I
can find out from a man in Tralee that works in a petrol
station.'

'No Covid?'

'No, me was tested. I'm clear – but the old people, dey die
frum it… It's terrible.'

Dessie drives on, and Jael sees the sweat gather on his forehead in tiny beads. She's glad now of Aswar, as he will get the worse of the smell.

The drive is pleasant as they pass through Glenbeigh, then the winding road to Killorglin, a small town with bustling streets and lots of people milling around. Jael thinks it's quaint. Dessie keeps going on about the "Puck fair", but Aswar hasn't a clue what he's on about so just smiles. Jael removes her feet from the dash as they head on for Tralee.

'Many a year I went to the Puck Fair. It was a great craic – lots of beer and women!'

Jael hides a smile when he goes red, like he thought he'd overstepped the mark.

'Well, Aswar,' he says, moving on, 'what brings your family to our shores?'

Aswar, not sure of the meaning of the question, looks at Jael for guidance but she doesn't know what to say to help him. He considers all for a moment.

'We had war in Sri Lanka. My grandfather was killed, my father and my muther were hurt when dey were young. Dey still hurt us Tamils even today so we got out. My father was sick and my muther wanted a better life.'

Dessie seems moved as he allows the boy's words settle for a minute. 'But you end up in Direct Provision?' He takes his eyes off the road and looks at the boy for a second.

'Yes, it's very bad…but we have no papers, we came without some papers…so dey do dat to us. I sleep like dis, and my muther and my father, dey sleep like this.' He demonstrates the lack of privacy for all by holding his hands apart to show the proximity of their sleeping arrangements.

Jael pats his leg and Dessie gives a knowing smile.

He gets diesel at a garage, while Aswar speaks to a man who is fixing punctures. This man is darker than him, and he listens intently as Aswar rattles away at a hundred miles an hour. The man nods and gestures in the air, letting the tyre fall to the ground. Aswar stops talking and looks down at it, like he doesn't know how it got to be so still. The man smiles, puts out his hand for Aswar to shake, which he does, and turns to come back to the van. Dessie is still in the shop paying for his diesel.

'Dey are in Ennis – de job's in Killarney – dey are gone now. Dey go to Ennis.'

Jael smiles at Aswar so he knows all is ok, and he smiles back.

Taking the road to Listowel, then on to Tarbert, Dessie is quiet and the air is cooler. He stops sweating but is looking serious and intense. They stop for ice creams at Jael's request, so Dessie allows her pay for three 99s. They sit at table used by coffee drinkers to eat them, and Aswar points out the window at the sky, wondering where the sun is gone. And then he listens intently to Dessie.

'So where is this uncle of yours?' Dessie bites his ice cream rather than licking it.

'He works in tyres but he is like my father, a forest man, like…chop chop!' He licks his ice cream, moulding it into a spire shape.

'Why did you come here?' Jael asks. 'Like, did your family think they'd get work in forestry?'

'Nah, maybe, but my grandfather was killed – dey killed him in front of my father.'

'Who?' Dessie bites his ice cream, leaving hardly any.

'The government soldiers came to his house. Dey drag him out onto the street and kick him an' call him bad names. My father is looking at dem – all de time dey kick him in de head, 'til he dies, and de blood is all over, and my father, he cries, he watches dis…and dey go way but dey come back many times 'til my father and uncles, dey are afraid to stay.'

Dessie finishes his ice cream first while Jael and Aswar play with theirs. They walk to the van. 'Do you know where in Ennis yer uncle is?'

'He is in Ennis – all I know.' He seems amused as Dessie sighs and throws his eyes to heaven.

The next morning, Jael awoke with a bad taste in her mouth. She turned in the bed to see Attracta standing at the bedroom door with a cup of tea in her hand.

'I heard you toss and turn, moaning in your sleep.'

Jael realised the tea wasn't for her. Attracta swished it around so much that it spilled over the sides, dripping onto the carpet.

'I'm alright,' she said, trying to sit up. 'What time is it?'

Attracta drank some of the tea, giving her the suspicious eye. 'You were late in. Obviously, school's out.'

Jael struggled to fix her pillows so she could sit straight. Her throat hurt and her mouth tasted foul.

'Can you get me the basin?'

'Jesus, you must be sick.'

'I am.'

'How much did he give you to drink?'

'Who?'

'Fucking Peter, that's who.'

'It wasn't Peter, it was yer man, Richard.'

'That pig!'

She left the room and came back with the basin, which she placed by the bed, within easy reach.

'You look wretched, girl. Do you want to get sick?'

Jael leaned over and vomited into the basin. It wasn't much at first but, when she wretched, it was colossal, like an erupting volcano, and her face went cold as the blood drained from it.

Attracta came to her bedside, placing her empty teacup on the table. 'What did those men do to you?'

Jael stopped vomiting, and Attracta gave her a tissue to help wipe the vomit bits from her lips.
'How do you feel now? A bit better?'
My head is throbbin'. He made me do things. His thing is all black and it's so big. He put it in my mouth – I can still taste it.' She spat into the basin. 'He spurted his stuff in my mouth.'
Attracta went to speak but stopped and didn't say anything for a minute – she just stared hard at her daughter.
'Did he put it in you?' she asked without emotion.
'No, he was going to but changed his mind.'
'The beast,' Attracta said, looking at her watch. 'I'll be late for the houses; I have to go. If you want aspirin, they're in the cupboard. Make some tea and toast and go back to bed, you can tell me all later.'
Jael watched her leave, sober and determined not to be late for her work. Peter wouldn't like it – he'd already threatened her and told her never to be late again.

The river is still, and the ferry makes an imaginary road as it glides through. Jael and Aswar go to the viewing deck but Dessie stays put, pensive, tired, and old-looking. Jael thinks he is in bad need of sleep. Aswar likes the view of the Clare coast right along the winding river. He points to their destination at Killimer and gasps. It's the first time Jael has seen the Clare coast, too, and she likes the way the river wrestles with the enormous predatory ocean beyond. Dessie is asleep when the ferry arrives at Killimer. He's confused and goes to fall back asleep but Aswar gives his arm a friendly puck. He jolts to consciousness and shakes himself like a dog before the beeping of cars behind make him move.

The backroads to Ennis are meandering and seem endless. Aswar is clutching his bag, and seems nervous, no doubt in anticipation of making an exit. Jael watches him twist and turn, alert to signs of any activity on the roads or the footpaths or on the by-pass as they approach the town. Dessie takes the exit to the town centre and looks surprised at how grandiose the place is, with some magnificent buildings, old narrow streets, and alleyways. It prompts him to announce, 'This looks good, Aswar.' Aswar smiles and clutches his bag tighter as Dessie pulls over. 'We could be traveling all day looking for your uncle, but I hope you find him. The best of luck.' He shakes the youth's hand.

Jael gets out the passenger side to allow him out, and he hops down onto the footpath, his bag held to his midriff. He hugs her, and she embraces his rubber body. Then he steps away, a little embarrassed.

'You are beautiful. I know you longer – I am in love, but you are too old for me – yet you are so young. As my father says, dat is de tragedy of life, it don't make sense ever.' And then he's gone, trotting without aim up the narrow street. He stops at the end and waves before turning left like he knows the town inside out.

Jael gets two take-out coffees and they sit and ponder Aswar's departure, with Dessie resting his hands on the steering wheel. She feels the tears gather but battles them back.

Soon after, they are on the motorway heading north. Dessie sucks on a fag while she raises her feet to the dash once again. They drive off the motorway, down a side road that twists and turns for miles 'til eventually they arrive at an inlet. Dessie hops out and reaches back for his fags. 'I won't be long.'

He's gone before Jael can respond. She watches him walk down the bank into only a few inches of water. It seems that way for miles – only a few inches of sea with tufts of bog grass, like the ocean has invaded the land. Dessie walks, unperturbed that his sneakers are getting wet. Sometimes, he splashes his feet, making the water look deeper than it is and he looks around like he's trying to remember something. He takes out his phone and takes photos, then puts it in his pocket again. Jael hopes he isn't going to walk to the headland where the ocean awaits. But he doesn't, he stops about fifty yards out and his body swells as he inhales, admiring the greenery, the odd-shaped rocks, and the nooks and crannies under the cliffs that hold small lagoons of green sea.

Watching you. Jael is keeping an eye. Once again you try to walk to America, but the water gets no deeper. You search the sky for help. A better life without Grandad and me. You told me about the seagrass and how it spread a trail across the Atlantic Ocean to Boston and New York. You would get married there and have a family with lots of money and security forever. Oh, Dessie, you with the pretty wife and all-American kids with shining teeth and baseball hats. The sandals you wore were soaked through so bad that Grandad made you take them off before getting back into the campervan. Wet shoes and wet dreams, I'd have followed you only for the fear of blood trickling down my legs. Would you have kept walking if you could? Like, if it were possible, would you have gone on, Dessie?

Kate

Attracta said no more about it that day or the day after. It was at the weekend, when Peter called down with a flagon of cider and some leftover cans of Heineken. He was in good spirits, as the papers for the sale of his properties were with the legal's, and now it was just a waiting game. He stuck out his chin when he informed Jael and Attracta of the pending sale, reassuring them that their tenure was safe for now. Richard had no immediate plans for this house or the others.

'He's gonna sit on them,' he said, all proud. 'That's what
they do, they buy them and sit on them 'til the price goes
up around the city, then he does them up and sells, or he
might even sell as is.' He drank a gulp of his cider, clearly
enjoying himself. Jael went to the fridge to get some
cheese, and he had to make way for her going and coming
back. He wasn't pleased with having to move twice but
Attracta, who sat at the end of the table near the kitchen
door, was ready for him.

'You'd think a big fella like him would find suitable
comfort in this city full of whores.'

Peter was taken aback and put his glass down on the table,
where it made an instant ring mark. He turned to face her.
'What do you mean?'

'A big fat-cat like him, reduced to raping young
schoolgirls.' She nodded at Jael.

Peter blushed and leaned back. 'There was no rape now. I
don't know what happened when I left the room but there
was no rape, Attracta.'

Jael shook her head but Attracta kept on. 'It is by age. Sex
with a girl barely sixteen is rape.' She was very concise,
and it undid Peter, who swallowed half his cider.

'I left her with him. She was grand chattin' away with him.
She was enjoying it. What am I meant to do, chaperone her
twenty-four hours a day? Look at the gear she had on –
drive a fella mad. He's only human, and she was all over
him.'

'I was not,' Jael said, 'I was just being nice – that's the
way I was brought up.'

'You shouldn't have brought her there, Peter, it's not
right. What he did to her isn't right. He damaged her, you
know, it's not right. He might be the big fella to you but he
won't be so big when I go to the guards about him.'

Peter went white. 'You can't do that; this whole place
depends on him. Think about it, woman, if he goes down,
we all go down, and you will be out on the street penniless.

He is our survival, and if these sales don't go through, were fucked, the lot of us.' He sat forward, shaking his head. 'Jael will do what she has to do to please him, do you hear me? The next time he wants to fuck her, he will fuck her.'

Attracta placed her elbows on the table, her head in her hands, sobbing. Jael looked at Peter, making direct eye contact. She thought she would meet steel but, instead, all she saw was fear and regret. He tried to smile at her, but it was a wasted effort to cover his helplessness, with tears of frustration building in his eyes to back it up.

'I lost everything in the investments and I can't afford to make an enemy out of Richard. If he says jump, I say how high, get it? We... You, are doing this to survive – whatever it takes, right?'

Dessie's first marriage was a disaster. Not just because Janet Johnston was mad but because she drove him mad, and it was I who introduced them. It was just after my time with Mr Dazzle. I got a job in the county council offices in Dun Laoghaire – it wasn't much of a job, doing shorthand and typing for the county engineer Mr Reid.

He was a pleasant enough man. He never married, but in those days, people didn't whisper as long as you kept yourself respectable, and he did. Mr Reid stayed in digs up in Clarinda Park. His landlady, Mrs Griffin, by all accounts loved him – like really loved him – spoiled him and made a packed lunch for him every day, as good as if not better than any doting wife. He was a fat little man, with a jowly chin, but a surprisingly young face. I always thought he had the wide eyes of a child. When he'd call me into his office, his eyes stretched so wide behind his spectacles that I thought it was a trick. But he was even-tempered and so gentle in his manner – if you had a problem, he listened, and you knew he was fair.

Janet Johnstown worked the other side of the room. She was younger than me, and though her dresses and skirts weren't particularly short, she somehow managed to show a lot of leg, even thigh on some occasions, which seemed to distract the rabble as they walked by. It came to Mr Reid's notice, though he never said anything to her but he did say it to me after promoting me to the role of office supervisor over the heads of others. It was my job to have a word with Janet, as it were. Mr Reid gave me two punts to treat her to an after-work drink in the Elphin hotel but she insisted we go to Lunny's pub downtown near the People's Park. It was her father's favourite pub, when he was being served, as he spent a great deal of time barred. He was a habitual drunk, all neat and respectable over the first few drinks but once he got onto the fourth or fifth, he'd let go, becoming increasingly messy – a habit that culminated in him annoying females, looking for kisses and what not. If he got loose with his hands, he invariably had to be thrown out.

Janet liked the pub, just the same as her father swore by it when he was sober. Brendan, the manager, always welcomed him back so her old man wouldn't hear a bad word about the place. I liked Janet then, she had a youthful exuberance, was thoughtful and funny, though she had all the traits that would later make her a thorn in our sides. But back then, she was innocent – lots of fun, if a little quirky, and I tried to see the best in her. She always walked slightly ahead, like she was forever in a hurry, which resulted in her turning her head to talk, and I couldn't help but study her narrow face, her pear-shaped nose, and sensual lips with blood-red lipstick making dark tunnels in her mouth. She insisted on buying the first drink, and I squeezed the notes that Mr Reid had given me, as if doing so eased my conscience. Her flowery dress dropped below the knee, which made things worse for me as I couldn't possibly use it as an example. Janet was preoccupied with Brendan, who was a fast mover and server. He filled shorts like it was some kind of a race and he'd be in line for a medal if deemed the fastest.

'He's a hunk,' she said later as she sipped her gin. 'Me da says they're all good-lookers in his family, includin' the oul wan and oul lad.' She laughed like she'd just said something really funny. 'But I won't be stayin' around here. Me da likes this place too much, and I won't be goin' where he goes, if yah get me, Kate. Nah, I think I might get away altogether, yeah know, get away from that awful atmosphere in our office. That prick Mr Reid,'—she lowered her voice— 'I hear he's ridin' that oul wan he has digs with. Did yah hear that, Kate?'

'Ah, no, I doubt it, Janet. Sure he hasn't it in him.'

'She has it in her.' She exploded into laughter, and the old men sitting at the bar all looked over such was her loudness.

'Now, now,' I said, 'none of that, we don't want to be spreading gossip.'

She quietened down and took a mouthful of gin. 'Yer no fun, Kate.' She laughed again, and I clutched my bank notes, knowing I mightn't spend them, as a few more drinks was all I would be able for. The thought of putting up with Janet any longer was way beyond the levels of my tolerance and patience but then she looked at me, all serious. 'Would you come to London with me? I need someone to come with me, Kate, you know, someone I can trust to look out for me, like. I don't want to end up on skid row in a big city like that. You wouldn't know who you'd meet and what they might do to you.'

'No,' I assured her, and 'No,' I said firmly so she wouldn't ask me again.

She got the message and changed the subject. 'I suppose I met worse than Reid. He's out of the office most of the time, and, sure, you're an angel.' She looked at me, her eyes glazed, like the gin had gone to her head.

'I try,' I said, somewhat sheepish. 'It's not easy but the girls are great.' I said it in a manner that she would know I was talking about "my girls," in a kind and nurturing way. I ordered a round using Reid's money, making sure to keep the change separate from my own cash. Janet was smiling now, enjoying the atmosphere, and seemed more relaxed, like she was stuck to the seat for the evening. Two more rounds came before she ran out of money, so it was easier for me then, although I was beginning to feel the effects myself, the gin burning my tummy, which it always did. I had to ask for a glass of water and ice to relieve the fire in my throat.

It was time for action. 'Janet, you are so attractive, the girls in the office love you but do yah mind if I'm honest with yah?'

She was stunned yet pleased that she commanded such attention – I could see that she wasn't used to it as she chewed on her bottom lip in anticipation.

'Could you leave your skirts or your dresses below the knee? Some of the males have commented, saying it's distracting.' I smoothed down my skirt with one hand. 'Would you mind?'

'Jesus, are you serious?'

I nodded. 'It's not a big deal, like, management don't know about it, or Reid isn't complaining, or anything like that.'

She lowered her head, her face disappearing as she stared at the carpet below the table. Her hair flopped after her, but then she straightened, as if to attention.

'Fuck 'em, I wear what I like to wear, there's no rule about that. Fuck 'em if I'm worried about 'em, Kate. Fuckers tellin' me what ta wear. I'll go buy a miniskirt, see how they like that.'

She shot to her feet and drank all her gin down. 'Fuck 'em.' And she was gone.

I still had a punt and change from Reid's money and was dizzy from the drink. Then Liz Cullen charged in the door like she owned the place, letting the light in, the nearest tables lighting up like she'd just shone a torch on them. She didn't see me and went to the bar, and Brendan was all attentive to her. They spoke for a moment before she leaned across the counter and kissed him on the lips. I was thinking of Janet and her comments about him, and how disappointed she would be now to find him necking with Liz Cullen, who was looking very pleased with herself. I expected her to look around or catch me in the corner of her eye but she didn't. I wanted to go up and tap her on the shoulder, the drink was shouting at me to fuck all of them and just go ahead and do it, but I couldn't. With tears swelling in my eyes, I stayed put, sitting there rigid like I was stuck to my seat. I drank another gin down, having paid once again with Reid's money. Heck, I decided I would just give him back the change. Liz was all talk with her lover and had the look of a girl who was very satisfied.

On the way for the bus, I thought again about all the stuff with Mr Dazzle, the way Liz had treated me. I was supposed to be her best friend but, when push came to shove, she was nowhere to be found – the opposite, in fact. She had done everything in her power to ruin me and my reputation.

The problems with Janet seemed to drift far away as I sat upstairs on the 7A bus going up the Noggin Hill. Liz had knocked Janet flat, her dresses and leg-showing paling into insignificance. Of course, I wasn't to know back then but Janet went on to fill a role that even Liz at her worst couldn't have managed.

I sat by the fire all morning with the television on, though with the sound turned down. Endless news shows – repetitive interviews with sports stars waffling on about stuff they find important but nobody in their right mind gives a damn about – followed by countless addresses by Richard Fanon about the aftermath of round one of the virus. He is mouthing the words but all I see are his lips moving like a goldfish, with a fat lady beside him miming in sign language, and gardaí in uniform all about. It's all official, very serious, but I know it for what it is: total drivel – every opportunity is a vanity exercise, where all opportunities must be taken when they arrive. Fanon smiles at the right time, allowing his voice shake with emotion at the right time, which is why I turn the sound down, to dull him, thus neutralising my own pain – the pain that has attached itself to me permanently. I awake each morning with it, I go to sleep each night with it. I'm cursed by my constant and terrible companion. I feel like I am being wrenched off my steel stand – at times I feel like I've been decapitated and some delinquents are playing football with my head. I make a good ball to be kicked into the air or volleyed into the net.

I drink hot drinks and use the heat of the fire to burn away the disease; the cancer cinders break like stale bread before my eyes. I'm thinking of Dessie and the disaster with Janet, and I'm admitting to his drink problem. No, I don't accept that she caused it – it was well there for many years before she got her claws into him.

Dessie and three pals went camping to Tralee. He was just fifteen years old, but his mates were older, except for Joe Tynan who was a year younger. It was a long and arduous debate, as to whether he should be allowed go, and one that Dessie lobbied passionately for. In the end he won the argument but, in hindsight, you might say he lost the brawl. It is what it is – I have come to terms with it now. Well, almost.

The bar was the length of the long room, and the barman was busy stocking shelves. He spent most of the time on his hunkers but stood occasionally to write things in a copy book. Murt was the oldest so he ordered the four vodkas. The barman didn't examine the entourage and continued to scribble in his copy book. Dessie gave a long sigh and Joe Tyan smiled and gave him a dig in the arm. Larry Bolger stood behind Murt like he was guarding his rear.

'What did you say you wanted, orange or lime?'

'Lime,' Murt answered.

'I want orange,' Joe Tynan said, then, realising he was bringing attention to himself, bent to tie his lace.

'Three with lime, one with orange.' The barman was fast, and the drinks appeared on the counter in double-quick time.

Joe didn't like his and made a face at the bitter taste. 'How dah fuck dah yah drink dis piss?' And he proceeded to swallow half of it, in complete contrast to Larry Bolger who just looked at his in wonder.

Murt stood over his like he was giving it the respect it deserved, showing his friends that's what you do – you give the drink respect by ignoring it for a while, acting like you didn't have it all by not giving it a blind bit of notice. Dessie was worse than Joe, knocking his back in two gulps. He laughed like his drink had travelled straight to his head, his eyes watering. Murt gave him a contemptuous look, then ventured to risk a sup of his own vodka, with Larry Bolger following suit.

The barman was buried away somewhere down the other end, lifting crates of mixers and sodas.

'I'm gettin' another round,' Dessie said to Murt and nobody else.

'It's piss but I'll drink it,' Joe told Murt, and Larry smiled like he had just won something.

'We have to keep the fare to Fenit.' Murt leaned over the bar to see if the barman was in view.

'Fuck Fenit,' Dessie said, 'I'm not spendin' me cash goin' there. What's in fuckin' Fenit?'

'A pier,' Murt replied, his tone stern. 'We can't stay here all day, we'll be locked. And we haven't the money. Nah, we gotta get out of here. Yer man will fuck us out if we stay too long. We're poxed he's servin' us as it is.'

Dessie thought about it and pulled a pound out of his pocket. 'How much is it?'

'One fifty-five,' Murt answered, seeing the barman's head appear again. 'Four more.'

The barman wasn't pleased to be disturbed from his tasks. He went red and rushed to the till. 'Three with Lime, one with orange.'

Dessie took out the change to go with his pound note and the barman collected it like a croupier in a casino, and off he went again, with Murt eyeing him all the way.

'I'm tellin' yah, Dessie, he will fuck us out – yer man is only fourteen.' He pointed at Joe, who didn't bat an eye and drank half his vodka in one go, with Dessie doing the same thing. Murt nursed his, and Larry now had one and a half drinks to Joe and Dessie's half.

'We better go to Fenit, lads, we have all fuckin' day.' Larry was serious, and even though he was wiry, the one thing he possessed was substance. Joe listened to him, nodding in approval, but Dessie was stubborn.

'Why don't we wait 'til he fucks us out, then we can go? We can find another pub later, what's the fuckin panic? Sure we can just sit here and chat about the young wans in the Noggin.'

'Yeah,' Joe said, lacking conviction.

'What young wans?' Larry asked. 'I've never seen Dessie with a young wan.' He laughed his wiry laugh, his head shaking.

'We'll be locked if we have any more,' Murt said. He lowered his drink, like he had abandoned all hope of teaching his compatriots how to drink properly.

'Joe and Larry have to get a round,' Dessie said. 'So we'll have two more and then I don't give a fuck. And what about Mary Browne, Larry, yeah? And all dose young wans from the tech in Dun Laoghaire? Yeah, dose young wans.'

'Me bollicks, Dessie, me bollicks.' Larry was getting tipsy.

'We're goin' to Fenit,' Murt said with authority. 'Go check the times, Larry.'

Larry looked up to him. Normally, he'd do whatever Murt asked. Not this time. 'No chance, I'm not goin' on me own. Joe, you comin' wit me?'

'Mehole, it's my round. In anyways, it's fuckin' miles to the bus station.'

Murt stiffened. 'It's just around the corner, you gobshite.' He shook his head. 'I'm tellin' yahs, he won't give us anymore. We were lucky to get these.' He swallowed his vodka whole, showing the lads it was time to go.

The barman made a beeline for them. 'I have to go to reception for a minute, will I top yahs up?'

Murt gave Dessie a cold look, and Larry smiled while Joe fiddled for his money.

'Yeah, ok,' Murt said, and the barman sprang into action.

8

Dessie went through various phases with drink. He could give it up when he wanted, and often he'd go months without a drop, then something would happen him and he'd go back on it big time. He'd meet up with his pals in the Victor Hotel or in the Graduate and go for it hell for leather. At that time, he hadn't got a girlfriend and that seemed to bother him but none of his mates had, either, except for Joe Tynan, who got married when he was nineteen. His girlfriend was pregnant, and in those days that was the way things were dealt with – it wasn't a matter of choice, it was a case of expectation.

Poor Dessie was on the road to nowhere, and I have to admit that he worried me greatly. Not that he bothered me in any way – even if he was plastered, he came into the house like a mouse and went to his bed. The very odd time I might hear him moan, and sometimes he'd be up half the night vomiting or, even worse, sitting in the living room crying and drinking whiskey 'til the early hours.

He got a job helping out on a building site down in Ballybrack, labouring and driving the dumper truck, but the foreman warned him time and time again for not turning up and going missing early on a Friday in a race to get to the pub. He got sacked so he had no money to drink, then he went off it, anyway, and even if I gave him money, he'd stay in to watch westerns on the telly.

Murt told me about the night they came back from Fenit, expecting to find Dessie asleep at the bar or in the toilet getting sick. There he was just as they left him, drinking vodkas and not a bother on him, listening to this older guy playing standards on an accordion and singing, 'Come down from the mountain, Katie Daly, come down the mountain, Katie Daly, come down from the mountain, Katie, do, can't you hear us callin', Katie Daly, we want to drink your Irish Mountain Dew…'

Dessie was singing along and Larry Bolger laughed 'til he was sick. Joe Tynan joined in, and Murt just threw his eyes to heaven like he was exasperated beyond belief. He ordered another round and they sat there for hours listening to the accordion player sing medley after medley. Later in the evening, Dessie spotted a girl sitting away from them down towards the hallway to the lobby. She wore a yellow rain mac and was super pretty, and he couldn't take his eyes off her. The lads tried to make conversation but he didn't respond, as it meant having to dilute his stare. The girl kept looking over, even laughing every now and again, like she found Dessie's staring amusing.

'Don't fuckin' stare,' Murt whispered, 'you will put her off yah.''

But Dessie was having none of it and his staring just got worse. Murt said he was like a man in a perpetual trance. They each lowered a stack of vodkas before the bar shut and it was time to move next door to watch the band 'Trend', who came out on stage in blue uniforms and belted out their numbers with great vigour. Murt and Larry were dancing on the tables, and Joe copycatted them near the end of the set. Dessie still drank vodka, still eyeing his girl, who now sat in the balcony. He stared at her and she smiled, like it was amusing her, and now and again she would have to break the chain, turning to talk to her companions. This was Dessie drunk, indulging in his fixation. He never spoke to this girl, yet one drunken night he told Murt that she was his true love.

Mr Reid was retiring and we had a party in the Pierre Hotel along Dun Laoghaire seafront. I asked Dessie along because I felt sorry for him. To be honest, I didn't want to be on my own the whole night, with all my work colleagues gawking at me. He brought Murt with him as a kind of back up. I put the two of them down as my guests, even if it raised a few eyebrows amongst the office crowd, as it was strictly work and partners only, but I said fuck them – most of them brought partners so who cares if I hadn't got anyone?

Dessie was on his best behaviour and looked smashing in his good jacket and trousers. Murt scrubbed up well, too, and most of the night he was chatting to Muriel McCabe, the young one from accounts. She was prim and proper and wore black-framed reading glasses. I have to admit that she was pretty, with rouge on her cheeks, mascara, and deep-purple lipstick. Dessie was dancing with different girls all evening and I knew he was drinking but he seemed fine and was thoroughly enjoying himself.

I went over to Mr Reid to congratulate him on his retirement but he was all emotional and out of sorts. When the band took a break, I could actually hear what he was saying.

'You know, Kate, they all think I'll take the gold watch, 'n' ride off into the sunset. If the truth be known, they think I've been havin' it off with Mrs Griffin. Oh, I know what they say, Kate, but the truth is, she doesn't interest me, not one bit. You see, I don't have a thing for women. Hush now, for God's sake, tell no one, but I'm relieved to finally tell someone.' He took a quick look around. 'I've lived a life in the shadows, slinking around the quays at night, meeting all sorts. Sometimes I was lucky to get out with my life, with this strange phenomenon "Queer Bashers". Imagine the sick people who hurt others because of the way they are? It's unimaginable, isn't it, Kate? No, I will probably go to Cork and live with my sister and my niece. They have a granny flat. I should most likely see my days out there. No, staying with Mrs Griffin wasn't bad at all, and coming to work each day… Oh, I'm heading into the abyss, I'm afraid.'

I was flabbergasted, looking around me to see if anyone else had heard. His words were shocking and the whole room went still for a second, before the music started up once more and his revelation got lost in the blasting sound. A little later, Janet Johnston came over. 'Come on, Mister Reid, give us a dance.' She shrugged her eyebrows at me. 'You can't be cuddlin' up to the staff even though yer leavin' us.' He got to his feet, slow and deliberate, like his hips were acting up or he'd been sitting in the one position too long.

'Yer bruther's a looker,' she remarked before leading Mister Reid onto the dancefloor, and I remember thinking, *You keep your grubby hands off my brother, you bitch*. But she danced with enthusiasm, and Mr Reid loosened up a bit to be fair, though he was all hands still and looked lost underneath the lights – the music was way too loud and modern for him.

Afterwards, Janet found Dessie sitting on a barstool and started chatting to him. He leaned in to hear her better, putting his hand around her back to steady her, and she accepted it. I knew then I was in trouble.

Mr Reid went to live in Cork. He said he would write and keep in touch but he never did – we never heard from him again, and I never found out what happened to him. Janet started to date our Dessie, who had just got a job selling cars in Gilmartin's up on Rochestown Avenue. This was all new to Dessie – he only got it because of some drinking buddy's connections. Soon, through whatever influence Janet had, he became a changed man. He gave up the drink and, instead of going to the Victor or the Graduate, they went to the pictures, or in the summer he would take her walking up over Killiney Hill. Sometimes they went on down the Vico on to White Rock beach, then onto Killiney beach. They would go down the military road and walk back the main road through Ballybrack. This really suited Dessie, allowing him to lose about a stone in weight. He looked fantastic, and so did Janet.

They became the right couple. When Dessie wasn't seeing her, he was content to sit in and watch his westerns. If I asked him how things were going, he'd smile and say 'Perfect'. He was selling loads of cars and Mr Gilmartin was talking about promotions and sales manager as a possibility. Dessie announced his engagement, and within months, he announced his wedding.

I can't say I got on or didn't get on with Janet. At work, she acted like nothing had changed. She still sat at the edge of her desk showing off her legs to the world, and she engaged in office gossip, even spread a rumour that Mrs Griffin had gone to Cork to seek out Mr Reid, but it wasn't true, yet it passed for true, as it was repeated endlessly, got dressed up, and people added on and subtracted from it over months of tongue wagging. When she called to see Dessie, she was altogether quieter, more respectful. She might sit with him, watching a VHS video, or sometimes he put on music and they cuddled on the sofa. She was always pleasant, if a little aloof in my presence, and pretended to like me for Dessie's sake. I didn't want to ruin it, either, for much the same reason.

They married on June 26th, which was Grandad's anniversary, which was made all the more poignant because Dessie didn't realise this when they booked the day. The marriage took place in the Noggin church, then to Killiney Castle, which was expensive but it was ok with me because they'd saved up and paid for it all themselves. Janet's father hadn't a cent, so he was hopeless, but the young couple took it all in their stride. Dessie liked the old man – they were always laughing and joking together. He broke his pledge for the occasion, and the two of them got stuck into small ones at the bar. It was like he was marrying Janet's father – the rest of the guests were invisible. He stayed sober enough for his speech, which is more than could be said for Janet's old man, who slurred and laughed inappropriately before pinching the bridesmaid's arse, and getting a slap for it, much to the upset of poor Mrs Johnston.

Murt saved the day with a funny speech, including how the boys had gone to Fenit and left Dessie behind in the bar, only to find him remarkably sober on their return, and how they all ended up dancing on the tables when 'Trend' played the music venue that night, and Dessie was the soberest of the crew. I saw Joe Tynan laugh and Larry Bolger hold back the tears as Murt related the stories of our Dessie in his wild younger days. He ended with a toast to the bride and groom, and Dessie was on his feet, proving that alcohol held no terrors for him.

'Ladies and gentlemen, may I propose a toast to Willy and my wonderful mother-in-Law Bernie. To my wife Janet, I thank her for accepting my request for her hand in marriage. I want to assure the Johnstons that I will always mind their daughter, and I will love and protect her with all my ability for the rest of my life.'

He gave Janet a squeeze around the midriff, and she beamed to her public while Willy lowered his champagne and looked for a refill, his wife putting her hand over his glass.

They moved into a council house down in Ballybrack, and Dessie loved it; it was a step up on the Noggin houses, very modern and the rooms were a little bigger too. Janet had a sneering 'it will do for now' attitude. She had her eyes on one of the four-beds in Johnstown, and refused to settle in, not liking the neighbours, swearing that if she had kids, they wouldn't see the street as the kids around were cheeky and wild, driving her mad with nick-knacks and throwing stones at passing cars. She wasn't going to settle. Dessie got the promotion and was now the sales manager in Gilmartin's. He got a lovely company car – a brand-new shiny Toyota Corolla liftback – which he showed off to Janet, but she wasn't amused, saying it wouldn't do if they had kids, and telling him to trade it in for a family saloon. I was there that day and Dessie's jaw dropped. He didn't change the car 'til she was pregnant on Sally, getting himself the estate version, and then I think he got a Carina. Sally and James, who came soon afterwards, could have all the room they wanted, or Janet thought they needed. He worked long hours, sometimes until ten at night, and when he got home, his dinner was dried out in the oven while Janet watched her shows she'd taped from earlier. She watched them when she had the kids in bed. Dessie would retrieve his meal and sit alone in the kitchen eating his dried-out food, mulling over the day.

Janet might pop in for a glass of wine. "Oh, yer home," was the best he got before she went back to her beloved soaps.

One day he called by and confided in me. "You know, Kate, I might as well live on my own sometimes. It's worse than you think, the loneliness is unbearable."

He began to visit me more, dropping by for lunch, and he often invited me to his place – it was like he wanted a witness to Janet's behaviour. To be honest, I was glad to go, my life had become lonely and difficult, and I rarely felt the good of things. One weekend, he invited me for Sunday lunch. Sally was full of beans, and little James directed all from his highchair. Janet was cheery but, as always, aloof to go with it. I could smell Dessie's uneasiness. She was a good cook and served up lovely roast chicken with roast potatoes. We had red wine, and even though I was driving, I had a couple of glasses – it was delicious.

The conversation was bland at first.

'I never go there,' Janet said. 'They're robbers, they catch you out on little things, like washing powder. The headlines are to grab your attention but they're really dear compared to Dunnes.'

I agreed with her in the main, it was hard to compete with Cornelscourt because the smaller outlets didn't have the buying power.

'How's business, Dessie?' I asked, thinking we could be in for a long road of supermarket prices and their good value.

'We're mad busy,' he announced, like that was it, "they were mad busy", and he didn't really want to talk further about it.

'Irene Burton was complainin' about you,' Janet said, going to the counter to get the wine bottle.

'Oh, yeah?' Dessie said, patting Sally on the head while lifting a spilled bit of roast potato back on her plate. James made blowing noises and drank juice from his cup. He seemed to be enjoying his role as a spectator.

'She says she bought a dud from yahs. I wouldn't pay her any attention normally but Joe said it was a heap of crap, too, so I got to wonderin'.'

'What does Joe Burton know about cars?' Dessie said, his tone gentle. He was still paying attention to Sally's plate – she looked up at him and smiled.

'Thanks, Daddy,' she said as he rearranged her food so it wouldn't slip off the plate.

'He's a fuckin' mechanic, or he was for years,' Janet said, ignoring the fact there were children present.

'I thought he worked in the garden centre,' I said, trying to appease the situation.

Dessie went red. 'She brought it back and we fixed it, we can't do any better than that. It was only a cheap run-around. It's a Fiat not a Merc.'

'Yeah, but it should fuckin' work.' She lowered her wine and poured herself more without offering me any.

Dessie sighed and drank his water down. 'Janet has a thing for Joe Burton. She thinks Irene is just an airhead.' He tried to distract us by talking to Sally but I could see Janet was fuming.

'At least he's a gentleman, he looks out for his family –
more than I get fuckin' here.' She stared me out of it.
Dessie was on his feet, bringing dirty dishes to the sink.
'Yer always on about him, Janet. If I didn't know better,
I'd think there was a story between you two.'
She drank her wine down and fixed on Sally for a moment.
James continued making his noises, oblivious to the
tension. 'Go wash yer hands, Sally,' she commanded. The
little girl twinkled her eyes at her and continued to play
with the dregs of her food. 'Now,' Janet screamed, and the
child, clearly rocked, got up and walked to the sink where
Dessie wiped her fingers with a facecloth. He did each
hand in turn, then dried them with a drying cloth. James
went quiet.
I drank my wine down but no more was offered so I stayed
quiet.
'Fancy a walk up over the hill, Kate?' Dessie sounded
more like himself now.
'Yeah, sure, love it.' I was on my way to help him with the
dishes.
'I'm not going there again,' Janet snapped. 'Why do we
always go there? I know…'—she mimicked Dessie—
'because that's where we played as kids. Fuckin' tired of
hearin' dat all the fuckin' time. You go with Sally, me and
James will go down the park. We can get some fresh air –
I fuckin' need it.

Dessie was quiet on our walk, preoccupied with Sally, who
ran ahead, her little legs working hard to get to the obelisk
at the brow of the hill. Later he held her hand as she
walked around the lower slabs on the wishing stone.
'What's up with Janet?' I asked as I gazed across Killiney
Bay, looking for small boats, then searching for ships on
the horizon.

'She's bored,' he said, picking Sally up and placing her on his knee. He sat back, taking in the late-afternoon sun and using the slabs of stone as a rest.

'She's carrying on with Joe Burton, behind Irene's back, and she thinks I don't know about it.'

'Really?'

'Yeah, I seen them at it in his car. They stop off in the church carpark on their way to get the take-outs on our card nights.'

'Wow.' I didn't know what to say. 'Did you follow them?'

'Nah, Irene forgot to order stuff so I went up for her – thought I'd surprise 'em – there was Joe's car bouncing away up beside the church.'

'What did you do?'

He shrugged. 'What can I do? What can I say? We have to think of the kids. I reckon it's a fling and will blow over, but sometimes, like today, I'm not so sure. Think it could be one of many but that's not what's wrong. Kate, you saw her at the table, she's itchin' for a row all the time, like she's lookin' for an excuse to get out.'

9

Kate eyes Dessie. 'Did you do what I asked you?'
'I did.'
He stands by the blazing fire. Kate is sickly looking but her face is still young, her hair flowing.
'I got you loads of photos, Kate. I'll put them on the laptop later.'
'Oh, good, you do that, Dessie.'
The cottage is bigger on the inside than it looks from the outside. Dessie sleeps downstairs at the front of the house while Kate takes to her sickbed at the rear.
'I'll fix you something nice for dinner.'
Kate smiles. 'Please do, I can't take another stew.'
He smiles back. 'You need to take a stroll down the beach – get some air.'
'I can't make it down the lane,' she croaks.
'I'll drive you down.'
She nods once. 'Yes, let's try that.'
He drives her jeep. It's old, and the insides are full of discarded water bottles. There is a rotten banana skin in the pocket of the door – it might be years old – and the seats are sticky, probably from the pile of wrappers on the floor, with more peering out from under the seat. Kate is laughing in the front as they drive down the narrow grass lane to the beach. Brown cattle, disturbed by the engine noise, stare at the jeep before moving about in an effort to relieve their discomfort. Dessie drives up through the gap and on to the beach proper. It is deserted, and Kate smiles when she sees this.
'Good man.' She encourages him to drive down to the water. The sea is magnificent in its calmness, as is the view over Blacksod to the saddle of Achill. Kate smells the cows in the country air and tastes the crystal salts of the sea.

'Stay where you are,' Dessie commands. He's at the boot, lifting stuff out, some of it heavy. The sun is high in the sky as he moves further up the beach, collecting stones. Then he lights a fire within the circle of stones. He uses wood he brought from the house, along with paraffin and firelighters. All the time, Kate looks on from the jeep window, smiling at the blaze. He also brought garden chairs, and the barbeque from the back yard. He's sweating, busy putting on sausages and rashers, with several pieces of chicken, along with a half-dozen lamb chops, all bought in Brogan's supermarket.

He throws a jacket around Kate's shoulders and moves the jeep so she gets the sun on her. Kate is fascinated by the line of light across the ocean, and the wave ripples that befriends and falls on the docile strand at Mullaghroe.

'This is just lovely,' she says. 'This is the business.'

Dessie hands her a paper plate and helps himself to one. He even brought knives and forks from the kitchen drawer.

'I need a break away from that damn television. That thing has my nerves shattered, with yer man Richard Fanon. You know he's goin' to be made Taoiseach? I'm tellin' you, Dessie, he's the next Taoiseach. No doubt. They're havin' a meeting next week, and he's the bookies' favourite. He's everything American – the business with his suits, his good looks. I can't stand to see him up there, like we're expectin' a hurricane. Him with his entourage, and yer man doin' the sign language, with all the officials standin' behind him, them warnin' us about Covid, and his government policies spreadin' the Covid in the Direct Provision, and the unregulated meat factories. Get me the gun, Dessie.'

Dessie smiles at her in an effort to get her to calm down. The first of the food is ready and he serves her, then himself. Kate is delighted, and she digs into the sand, giving ballast to her feet as she holds the paper plate on her knee.

'Fuckin' politicians,' he says. 'Wankers all.' He laughs, serving more sausages and burnt pieces of chicken.

'A feast,' Kate says, throwing the jacket off her shoulders and allowing it drop to the sand. 'Weird how everyone finds these suited fellas respectable, like the suit is the knight's armour in modern times. Personally, I wouldn't trust any of 'em. If they're asked a hard question, they won't answer it, they just give a speech themselves, usually about somethin' off the point, and folk are happy with that? It's like they think the populace is thick.'

'Maybe they are, Kate.' Dessie puts a lamb chop on her plate. 'It is beautiful here at Mullaghroe.'

Kate smiles, like Dessie's voice is stoking her fire. 'Oh, yes, always reminds me of Grandad's sparse picnics, remember them, Dessie?'

'I do, the picnics without food.' He laughs.

She looks at him. 'Grandad thought some fruit, followed by a drink of coke with a cream cake constituted a picnic. We'd be ravenous, wouldn't we?'

'I nearly ate the paper bag he had it all in.' He laughs again.

The sun is sinking out over the bay, lying red by the cliffs of Achill. Kate feels the cool breeze, and the sea goes quiet, like it wants sleep.

The fire is dying as evening comes. Kate, her face alight, stares into the embers, reflective, the gentle waves apologetic as they hit the shore.

'The modern world is so full of crap.'

Dessie is tidying up, loading the jeep. He stops to listen to her.

'How come everyone's a scholar now?'

She's barely visible beyond the smoking embers.

'It wasn't like that in our day – only the brightest and the best got to go to college.'

'And the wealthy, Kate, it was nothing to do with the brightest or the best – a lot to do with dosh, and how much you had of it.' He throws his chair into the rear of the jeep, like he's trying to make a point.

'Sure, yeah, but now I go on Facebook and every kid has graduated. Young lads and young ones all in the garb – where will they all end up? Many of them emigrate and end up flippin' burgers down in Sydney.'

Dessie stops what he's doing and walks over to be near his sister. 'This is capitalism, Kate, its nothing to do with doing well, but to do with expectations. They want you to go to college because it's a way of milking your dreams. They want you to be a high achiever with a low salary so you can borrow your dreams from the banks who own you, and you pay a mortgage for most of your life. If they get their way, you will be paying student loans, too. It's called climbing the rainbow to find there isn't a crock of gold, then you die like everyone else.'

Kate smiles. She sees the white waves ripple close by as the tide approaches. Dessie helps her into the passenger seat, avoiding the plastic bottles and wrappers at her feet.

Dessie is busy again, relighting the house fire so Kate won't be cold. The television is on but the sound is mute, and there's Richard Fanon, giving a lowdown on the Covid, terrified of a second wave, blaming people for partying in their homes and for not social distancing properly. Kate reads the subtitles for the hard of hearing, imagining the dourness and danger in those unregulated meat plants.

'Richard wants to look over his properties.' Peter was blasé, and Attracta gave him the evil eye.
'So when's he coming?'
'Shortly, but he won't stay long – we will move on to number fifty-two as soon as he's done here. I'll show him upstairs first.'

'Jesus, Peter, the place is manky – you should have said. And what about Jael? She'll have a stroke.'
'No, she won't. Where is she, anyway?'
'In her room, why?'
'I need to talk to her, that's why – we need to clear up stuff so there'll be no messin' around or misunderstanding.'
'What do yah mean?' She watched him walk down the hall into Jael's room. He didn't knock on the door. Jael sat up from where she'd been lying on the bed, over the bedclothes, listening to music on her headphones. She took then off.
'Richard is coming by to inspect the house,' Peter said.
'He wa—'
'This is of interest to me because…?'
'You know well, Jael, the stuff you told Attracta. I don't want you pestering him. He thought you were up for it – you know Richard's a gentleman, just like his father, he wouldn't do anything unless he thought you were up for it. He must have got his signals mixed up. Jesus, you were dressed like a whore, you can't deny that Jael.'
'You don't get it, Peter, I don't give a rat's fuck how I was dressed. He forced me to do stuff, and any amount of lick-arsing from you won't change that. But I'll stay in here, so don't bring him in and we will be grand, won't we?'
'He has to see the whole house – he has to see what he's buying.'
'Jesus, ok. Give me the heads up and I'll go to the kitchen or the living room, alright? Do your worst, Peter.'
Peter returned to the kitchen, where Attracta gave him a mug of tea. He paced the floor, tetchy and nervous.
'Why don't you sit easy, Peter? It's not God who's callin' by.'
'No, but he can make or break me. He's sendin' his surveyor over in the morning. If they find anything wrong structurally, I'm gone.'

'There is nuthin structurally wrong, for fuck's sake, Peter, you know that.'

'I know, Attracta, but maybe I should send Jael out, give her some money. Would she go down to the city shopping? But then he might be mad. He likes Jael – expects her to be here.'

'Dirty cunt,' Attracta snapped. 'I'm tellin' yah, Peter, if he lays a hand on her.'

'On who?' Jael asked, walking into the kitchen, wearing jeans with a woollen sweater. She moved to the back door and looked out over the lawn to where the wild grass grew, battling with a line of vegetables for space. She saw her underwear on the clothesline and wondered if she should remove them, but it was too late – the bell rang – and there was safety in numbers.

Richard Fanon stood in the hallway. Even in the low light you could make out his handsome features. He wore a light, full-length winter coat, and when he walked into the kitchen, he eyed Jael and Attracta. As he rubbed his hands, his beaming smile lit up his whole face – the smirk was part of him, it belonged to him, and it didn't matter if he was happy or sad or angry, it stayed there.

'So, which wall fell down, Peter?' He laughed at his own joke. 'I hope we have your votes on Friday week?' He looked earnestly at Attracta, who went to speak but bowed her head instead. 'We need the young people to vote,' he said to Jael, who ignored him and went to the back door to check on her washing again.

'This is the living room,' Peter said, his voice trembling. 'Come on and I'll show you around.'

On his way out, Fanon stopped and turned towards Jael, his smirk stuck firm. 'You know, some people worship me. They love what I do. I change things. If the well is empty, I fill it, if the factories are gone, I bring new ones. I give people hope, and you think you can ignore me, both of you? But I'll have you know, girl, you don't have a say.

Nor do you.' He looked at Attracta, who tried to speak but once again couldn't find the words. He clicked his fingers. 'I do that, Peter jumps. I feed him or, at least, I will feed him, and you two, once this deal goes through, and it will. I will own him, and I will own both of you. Remember, I click my fingers, you will do what I say, what I want, ok? Got that, ladies?' He said ladies in snide fashion, and Attracta started to cry, holding her side as if she'd suffered a terrible, sudden pain.

Dessie brings Kate her breakfast of scrambled eggs and toast on a tray and sits with her as she eats. She is complaining about the television again.

'There he is again, that bloody man in his dapper suit.'

'Don't be mindin' him,' Dessie says. He turns the sound down.

'He's wavin' his arms at me now – he's markin' my card. It wasn't enough for him to kill off the elderly, he's after the rest of us now.'

'I blame the opposition for not bringin' him down.'

Kate stares at Dessie, silent, like she's thinking about it, then she shakes her head. 'There is no opposition – only mouthpieces. They took the country in the counter revolution. They took it with guns and bombs, and we need guns and bombs now, it's the only way we will ever get it back off 'em. They will fight 'til the death to keep control and it will be very messy and bloody, Dessie.' She groans. 'I don't know if my stomach could take it – not now, anyhow.'

Dessie doesn't reply.

'We will have to rob a bank, like, though the money's no good to me now, but for the craic. Like, you have the gun in that paper bag – don't deny it, I saw it when you came here. Did you get that off the blind man?'

She sounds lively, and Dessie mumbles something.

'We can rob the Bank of Ireland down the town. Jack Oliver will turn in his grave – he did all his banking there. It would be a real thrill – one last final thrill – telling the staff to put up their hands and snatching the cash.' She laughs. 'The guards will give us a good chase. We should head out of town in the opposite direction, then ditch the getaway car and return in our own jeep. It will work. Do you think it will work, Dessie?'

She eats all her food and Dessie looks pleased. He is on the way to the sink. 'How do I feel about robbin' a bank?' He laughs. 'Oh, good, it will cheer you up Kate, so I like the idea.'

Jael called the ambulance at 2 a.m. Attracta had fallen again, this time hitting her head off the back step. The door to the garden was open and she'd been smoking fags and listening to the radio. The blood gushed from her forehead where the skin had come loose in the shape of a plaster around a neat round hole formed by a hard edge. Peter came downstairs, woken by the screaming and wailing, then the arrival of the ambulance. They took the semi-conscious Attracta away to CUH – Cork University Hospital – and Jael went with her. Peter slipped her some cash to get a taxi home, for which she was thankful. The duty doctor directed her into the waiting room while he examined her mother, and despite Jael's protests, she ended up there, sitting alone, looking at magazines but not reading them, as it was impossible to concentrate. After an hour, the doctor appeared and announced that Attracta had severe concussion and would need to stay the night. They would examine her again in the morning. Jael hailed a taxi and was home within ten minutes. The house was quiet – not a sound – and she presumed Peter had gone back upstairs so she went to the kitchen to tidy up. There he was sitting at the kitchen table nursing a whiskey.

'Well, will she live?' he asked, brazen.

Jael filled a bucket and added floor cleaner, then started to mop the blood. 'They're keeping her overnight. I'll ring in the mornin'. She glanced at the kitchen clock. 'In a few hours, I mean.'

'She's getting worse,' he said, lowering the whiskey. Then he was up to the press to freshen up. 'Do you fancy one – yer nerves?'

'No, not for me,' she said. 'I'll make tea before I get to my bed.'

With most of the blood mopped up, she opened the back door to clean the step.

'Close that, it's fuckin' freezing.'

'I'm nearly done,' she barked.

'Keep yer hair on, will you. You know, some day she will fall and never wake up. Her head will crack open and she'll bleed to death.'

'Jaysus – cheer me up, Peter. I left the change on the counter from the taxi,' she added to help soften him.

'Keep it – I have somethin' else for you.'

She looked at him and flinched inside at the sight of him starting to masturbate.

'How's about a bit for me?'

'Not if you were the last man in the world.' She tried to be brave but he was deadly serious.

'You did Richard's – now how about mine? We'll call it quits for the taxi.'

She could see the blood build in his head, and new crease lines appeared as he stared at her. She broke eye contact, left the mop against the counter, then dropped to her knees, hardly able to see through the welling tears.

10

Jack Oliver headhunted me from the county council. To be honest, I was glad, as it was after Mr Dazzle became public. I was the talk of the office. It wasn't so much they knew anything but it was what they thought they knew that bothered me – whispers everywhere, conversations ending abruptly when I came near, hands covering mouths at the other side of the room as words were hidden. I thought I was living in a dark, surreal dream.

Dessie was having his troubles, too. Janet made him leave the house, even though she didn't openly have anyone else. He saw his kids at weekends only, and even then, he had to make up camp beds in his tiny flat – all in all it was a disaster. He started to drink again, heavier than before, and his job was on the line. So when Jack Oliver asked me to go work for his engineering firm, I took the opportunity, handing in my notice and telling nobody. I left on the Friday, acting like it was any other day, saying the usual 'Enjoy the weekend' junk before leaving and getting the bus home alone, never to return. No leaving party for me, just a weekend preparing to start a new job in a whole new world.

I offered Dessie his old room back but he wouldn't take it, saying it wouldn't work with the kids coming to stay and the neighbours, like old Mrs Stubbs, wanting to know about his failed marriage. The kids would hear all sorts from her grandkids who had moved in after her daughter's husband left her to go to England – the irony of it. Dessie's bedsit must have been bad as he never had the guts to show the place. It was off the Meath Road in Bray, that's all I know – it's all I ever knew. When I asked the kids about it, they'd say it was ok and left it at that. I knew by their tone and Sally's expression that it wasn't great, that she was just being brave about it.

My mind was full of Dessie back then. One night, he came by my house by mistake, so drunk he thought he still lived there. He frightened the life out of me opening the hall door with his key at two a.m. I was sure I was being burgled. I grabbed the old sports cup that belonged to Grandad from the top of the dresser in my room and abseiled down the stairs with it raised over my head, ready to strike a deadly blow. But there he was conked out at the foot of the stairs – my Dessie rolled up in a ball, sleeping like a baby, a faint smile on his face. I wanted to throttle him, of course, for giving me such a fright but I didn't, I made him coffee, and he said he was hungry. I was worried about him as his face was flushed and he'd put on stacks of weight, and he smelled of BO. The occasional loud fart didn't help, but he laughed when he did them, just like he did when he was a kid.

'I miss putting them to bed, Kate.' He was starting to sober up and his words weren't as slurred. 'But you know the thing that really gets me?' I stopped stirring the scrambled eggs. 'If anything happened, like there was a fire or somethin', I wouldn't be there to save them.' He started to cry, and so did I – there we were, the two of us, in that tiny scullery, crying our eyes out, a right pair of eejits. The more Dessie spoke, the more he cried, and the more he cried, the more I did.

'What if I can't save 'em?' he blurted.

I burned his eggs and stirred them frantically trying to save them – the smell was everywhere.

He slept in his old room that night. When he woke really early that morning, his face was so pale and he drank his tea like it was water, getting up and going to the scullery to refill it several times, unable to eat. I offered to make him sausages but he went green so I rang Gilmartin's to tell them he had a bad cold. Old Gilmartin was rough with me, basically calling me a liar, which I was. He grunted at me

and didn't say goodbye properly. Dessie knew his job was
gone. So did I but we said nothing about it, such was the
state of him.

'Do you want to go lie down?' I was heading for my bus.

'Yeah, in a minute,' he said, looking grey and old.

'You will sleep it off. Take a few hours, love.'

He looked at me through glazed eyes, then down at his lap,
like he was ashamed. 'I drank whiskey. Lots of fuckin'
whiskey. That's why I'm in this state.'

'You will be fine.' I shut the door and closed my eyes for a
second, trying to make sense of his last expression but
there was no time – if I missed this bus there wasn't
another for fifteen minutes. I passed the sitting-room door
and thought of Grandad. If he was still around, what would
he say to Dessie? Would he encourage him or take him on,
hit him a punch to wake him up? Grandad was all mouth –
a big softie underneath. I could see him putting his arm
around Dessie's shoulder and listening to him bleat it all
out tearfully. That was Grandad, and even though he might
have exploded occasionally, he was really soft hearted –
that was his true self.

I thought I heard the piano keys but it turned out to be a
noise from outside. I wanted to open the front door and
rush for my bus, but I was compelled to stay as I
remembered his music. It was Grandad's own tune, the
one he played, where he'd say, 'It's just a little something
I'm working on meself.' It had a beautiful lilting sound,
and its gentleness suited the moment.

The bus was pulling into the terminus, and the tune
followed me across the ring – his own gentle song: do dah
da da dah…dah dah dad da dah… He never finished it, nor
did he ever give it a title, but that tune lived on in my
heart. Did Dessie know it? Or hear it, maybe? Or did
Grandad only play it for me? I made a mental note to ask
Dessie about it.

I tried not to think anymore of him as the bus thundered towards Rochestown Park. I studied the rows of houses, the older two-stories on my left and the spacious bungalows on my right. All those lives: the families, the minutes, the hours, the days, the weeks, the months, the years; the dreams – all taking place in these little pigeon lofts. I thought of Mr Dazzle and started to rationalise it all but it was impossible as it didn't warrant rationalisation. It only needed catharsis. It needed telling. Besides Dessie, who was there to tell?

Elizabeth was long gone, and I had taken to walking the seafront alone. I loved the late September evenings and the streetlamps reflecting on the water. I was nearing Sandycove when I saw him, Mr Dazzle, lying on the ground by a park bench. His face was leaking blood, his nose bashed in, and he had cuts on his forehead. I rushed to his side, looking around to see if anyone could help but the evening was quiet. A dog walker passed but just stared as I tried to lift the poor man by the shoulders. He was muttering incoherently but I kept asking him what it was he wanted to say, and the gibberish continued 'til I got him sitting on the park bench.

'I know them, I know who they are.'

'Sssh, sssh, I'll go get help, call yah an ambulance.'

'No, no ambulance, I'll be alright. It's my hips, they kicked me in the ribs and hips, and in my face.'

'Who are they?'

'The fat fella from York Road, with his cronies. I know them, I know who they are. They hang about here. They are queer bashers but I'm not queer, though they don't know that.'

Blood spat from his mouth as he spoke. 'I was sitting here minding my own business. They passed me by at first but they doubled back and…wham!'

They did a right job. I tried to stop the blood coming from his nose, gushing again like he'd been shot. I got him to his feet. In fairness, he made a valiant effort, all the time moaning, spitting, speaking lucidly, before relapsing into his jabbering again.

I used his key and got him into the hallway. Of course, his flat was on the upper floor but he helped as best he could and I got him there after long rests on each landing. I wondered what his neighbours would make of all the blood. The place was eerily quiet, and nobody seemed interested in checking out all the fuss. No doors opened, even just enough to allow eyes to peek out.

The flat was small, the place full of clutter. He had a cooker, a fridge, and a battered-looking television over by the window, which allowed good views of Dublin Bay. His rear window overlooked an overgrown garden, a maze of walls, and thin looking apple trees. His sink was stained brown, and his cutlery had the remains of food stuck like they were never washed properly. I got him on to his two-seater and convinced him to hold his head back as I searched for a handkerchief. All I could find was a dirty dishcloth but it did the trick. He held it tight for me, which was good – and it wasn't too long before the blood stopped altogether.

'You should go to the guards,' I said, wiping his chin with the other end of the dishcloth.

'What will they do?' He was more coherent now.

'They will arrest those brats.' I was still wiping his chin. He didn't protest.

'Waste of time. The guards know all about them. They bash queers every night of the week, and the guards turn a blind eye.'

'You don't remember me, do you?'

'Should I?' He moved his head, the action slow, his pain obvious as he tried to see me better. 'I don't have a clue. Do I know you?'

'Myself and my friend Liz took your photo outside of Joyce's tower. Ah, it's ages ago, probably four years back.'

'Oh… I don't remember, sorry, my memory is very bad, but if you say so.'

'Have you any plasters or bandages?'

He shook his head. 'No, I never need them. I don't have any.'

'Where are you hurt most? Is it your side?' I looked at his side.

'Yes, my hips, though my ribs took the brunt of their kicks. I'm afraid those blighters knew what they're doing.'

'Can I contact anyone, friends or family?'

Mr Dazzle went quiet, like he was considering something. 'No, my sister doesn't like to be disturbed, not at this hour of the evening. I'm afraid I don't know my neighbours – they are rather reclusive. There is just me, really.'

I stayed with him for another hour, making him tea and holding the dirty dishcloth over his nose when it started to bleed again. I got the bus back to the Noggin, worrying if I had done the right thing. There was a payphone in the hallway of the building – maybe I should have rung for an ambulance, or even asked if he had a doctor, but I didn't, I left him on the two-seater in a state.

The next day, I bought several morning papers on the way to work and listened attentively to news on the radio in the office. Nothing, no mention of an assault in Dun Laoghaire or Sandycove, so I presumed Mr Dazzle was fine, or perhaps he just died where I left him. Like, who would have known? Nobody, unless his sister got in touch or called by to see him, though that didn't seem likely.

A tall young man, with pudgy cheeks and a funny beard that was mostly under his chin, let me into the hallway, and I tapped on the door of the flat but received no answer so I knocked again and waited. A woman leaving the flat opposite asked me was I alright, and I gave her my best smile and told her I was. She worried me more, then, by saying 'He's a quiet man – never see him – hope he's not dead in there?'

She laughed and disappeared down the stairs. Then the door clicked open and there he was, in his dressing gown and looking much better, though a little confused to see me standing before him. He was edgy and nervous, and I sat on the two-seater while he pretended to look out the window.

'I didn't hear you. I was in the dark room – I converted the spare room. Photos are my thing.' He pressed his face against the windowpane but the evening was lost – it seemed to rain on his excuse to look into space.

'Nothing left of the day. I hate this time of year – it isn't summer, nor is it winter – the world is confused, and me with it.' He smiled as he crossed the room, then fiddling with something on the mantelpiece that caught his attention.

I was taken with the coldness of the fireplace and wondered what the room would look like if the fire was lit, fire flicker making shapes across the old carpet and along the battered walls. No, it hadn't been lit for a long time.

'I dropped in to see how you were. I was worried for you, to be honest.' I tried to sound eager.

He stopped playing with whatever he was playing with. 'That is so kind. I'm much better today, getting the movement back in my legs – my hips.' He did a sort of swift imitation of the twist to show me how he was improving. 'I looked out earlier. No sign of those thugs along the seafront. Maybe they will retire now with the weather changing.'

'Can I use your loo?'

He looked at me like I'd asked him something he just couldn't countenance or was physically and emotionally unable to do.

'Can I use the toilet?' I asked, smiling.

'Through that door on the right.' He was very precise.

I found it, and there was a dreadful smell – not of human waste but something else, like milk had been spilled and had gone sour. When I came out, I noticed his bedroom door was ajar. I peered through the crack and saw him standing over his bed where hundreds of photos were spread out but I couldn't make out what they were or who was in them – they were a blur.

He came bursting through the doorway, 'You didn't see those photos?' His eyes were wild.

I stepped back. 'No.'

'Are you sure?'

I was back in the main room, heading for the two-seater to pick up my coat. He was beside me, and I could smell the sweat running down his body. The air around him tasted of ink – a chalk smell – and I could taste that musty stuff from my old classroom.

'My sister is doing me out of my inheritance because of my love of photos. Can you credit that?'

'I'd best go. I'm glad you are on the mend. My brother is waiting for me downstairs – he has a car.'

'Really? You never mentioned him when you arrived. I was going to make us tea.'

The dressing gown tie was loose and fell away as he turned. 'She doesn't like my fascination with boys. She says it's unnatural – it's uncouth. What do you think?'

I saw that he was naked and could feel his arousal as he came really close, his chin almost touching mine.

'She won't believe me when I tell her that I like the ladies, too – she says I'm spoofing. That's why I don't live at home in the family home – my mother's house.' He gritted his teeth and shook his head, and in a second, I was pinned to the cushion.

I fought him. He wasn't strong, still weak, and sore, so I concentrated on his ribs and hips, kicking and punching as best I could. Then he hit me with the living-room lamp, right in the centre of my forehead. The room swirled, and I couldn't get my bearings. He undressed me below the waist and raped me, and then he made me turn over and raped me again, from the rear. He repeated this process, and sometimes he stopped to take a drink – he had a bottle of scotch on the kitchen shelf. He'd sit there for a minute, staring at me, talking endlessly, mostly to himself. At one stage I thought I heard him sing.

11

The guards arrested him but he denied everything. And even though they charged him, his family got him a smart lawyer who threatened to make mincemeat of me on the stand, so I dropped the charges. When I found out that I was pregnant, I got the night boat to Liverpool, where I stayed at Mrs Archer's B&B – she kept a good house for expectant mothers. It was in a rough area but I remember her as a warm, jolly person, full of empathy for my suffering.

I got the bus to the hospital, where I received the all-clear for my procedure. A few days later, I arrived at the clinic – a big old house with a gravel drive – nondescript in its ordinariness, with a few cars parked within its railings. A man stood by the garden wall, heaving on a cigarette like he was dreading something happening yet he knew that he had no control over it. The staff were efficient but seriously cold, and the waiting room was the worst I'd ever waited in, even worse than the Public Dental clinic on Patrick's Street where they made us wait for the butcher dentist when we were schoolkids, although I didn't hear anyone screaming like I did there as the butcher went at them with his cruel instruments.

What made this place worse was the expressions on the faces – they all held a kind of dead look. Folk didn't seem to think it fitting to chit chat. There were various groups: a mother and her daughter; a husband and wife – I noticed their wedding rings – and two single women opposite me. The man who was smoking outside appeared and sat with the mother and daughter; they didn't speak or even exchange glances. I was last. The magazines were way too old and out of date to distract me, so I just sat and waited, trying not to make eye contact with those around me.

The numbers dwindled and, eventually, it was my turn. They did what they do – the nurse was cold, though the

doctor was warmer but really serious. I was left to wait for
over an hour before they discharged me – the last to leave
the building. I went for the bus back to Mrs Archer's,
scheduled to leave for home the following morning.
Suffice to say, I wasn't glad or relieved that this rapist's
child was sucked out of me. I was only glad that it was
over. Nothing else crossed my mind. It was over, and all I
had to do now was get over the shame of the whole
experience.

Everything was cold – the bus was freezing, as were all the
folk on it. It was a bitter evening in Liverpool, and the
place looked tired. All was wretched, with no buzz about
the city, even though the neon flashed bright and the cars
had their dimmers on. Any warmth seemed to bleed into
the atmosphere.

Mrs Archer made me tea and held my hand while I cried,
then gave me a hot-water bottle to bring to bed. Two new
girls arrived, both nervous as they studied me. I tried to
shake myself up for them but couldn't, no matter how I
tried, and my tears kept coming in floods.

When I came home to Dublin, Dessie was a new man.
He'd met Bridie and his life was good again. She was
older than me but wore it well. She had a history, with
seven grown-up children and ten grandchildren, and was
stunning for someone with that kind of a background. Her
marriage was a disaster but, as is with Irish Catholics, she
stayed put for the kids, only leaving her husband much
later when the kids were grown.

Gilmartin still allowed Dessie sell cars for him but no
longer employed him directly. Dessie sold Bridie a car,
and she rang to tell him how happy she was with it. Soon
they were meeting for drinks and going for walks up over
the hill. He was beaming, greatly taken with her. Bridie
wasn't like Janet in any way, having none of her feistiness
or bad temper. She was safe and secure, experienced, and
smart, with a good boutique business in Blackrock and her

own house up in Flower Grove, where Dessie spent most of his time. He was way younger but they looked great together – you knew there was a deep affection between them.

For ages they lived a life in the distance but I met her a few times with Dessie. She was kind and nice, and easy to get along with. I first got to know her when Jack Oliver hosted an open weekend in Belmullet. Loads of would-be takers let him down and, in the end, it was just me, Jack, and Dessie and Bridie, and it worked out surprisingly well. Jack was in his element, doing his beach snorkelling thing and hosting his BBQ on the beach, with lots of wine and champagne.

We were joined by Joyce McKenna, an assistant bank manager originally from the North, but now living and working in Belmullet. Jack had a thing for her, and she for him. She was an awful-looking yoke, with flaming-red hair and freckles. Dessie found her hard, and that says something as he was a real people person. She was weeny and sour, with brittle bones under sagging skin, twisting her mouth this way or that depending on her opinion on what was happening around her. Jack was jovial, always loud, wanting the ensemble to have the craic. Joyce, however, looked at us with an accusing eye, thinking we all had a thing for Jack's money and we didn't deserve the lavishness he threw at us. She was a snob, figuring Dessie and I weren't good enough for her or for Jack, who carried on oblivious to her moody silences or her raw dagger expressions.

Bridie gave me a few "Who's yer wan?" looks. She winked at me, then sang a song – a lovely ballad from her home village in West Cork. The words were shockingly sentimental and it brought tears to Dessie's eyes, and Jack was enthralled by it. Bridie was a fine singer but Joyce thought she was mad to be singing on the beach and

looked around to see if any stragglers might be offended
but we were all alone.

By now, the evening had taken hold and the last of the sun
revellers had left for home. Bridie took hold of Dessie's
hand as they walked down the beach towards the rocks at
the end, the sea in tune with them, the soft waves
representing harmony for the first time since I could
remember. He looked happy, and I bowed before the gods,
wishing this to be everlasting. I vowed to make things
happen in my own life so that I could enjoy happiness too.
Joyce didn't see the world that way, bitching at Jack to go
back to the cottage to break the party up.

'I don't know, I fancy a late swim.' He wasn't big or
robust, slight in appearance, his cropped hairline making it
more pronounced, but when he took off his shirt, his chest
was impressive, with a lot of hair, and female-shaped
nipples.

Joyce was on her feet, wagging her finger at him. 'Don't
be daft, Jack, you've had too much to drink.'

'I heard it yesterday; it was on the radio news – you only
live once.' He was gone, running to the water's edge. With
a splash, he was immersed in three feet of beautiful
refreshing seawater.

Joyce had a head on her like someone thrashed her with a
dustbin lid--she wasn't impressed. head bowed, she went
stomping up the grass lane, with Jack roaring out her name
from the water. She kept going to make a point, and he
kept shouting after her 'til she disappeared. Dessie and
Bridie were on their way back, still holding hands, then
swinging their arms through the air like some sort of
linked pendulum. Jack dived under and came back up with
water gushing off his head.

Although it was summer, Jack lit the fire at night as the
temperature dropped even on the warmest of days. We sat
around the large kitchen table, with Jack pouring red and
white wine. He tried to organise a game of 'Newmarket'

but neither Joyce, who was still sulking, or Bridie wanted to play. Bridie said she'd never heard of the game and wasn't in the mood to learn, as she felt tired. Jack, who was normally so calm and collected, got irked and poured himself an extra-large glass of wine. Then he got up and poured an ice-cold beer from the fridge to nurse alongside it, much to Joyce's displeasure.

'Are you drinking both?'

He smiled, twinkling his eyes to annoy her further.

'Isn't it desperate the price of houses now,' Bridie said in an effort to divert the conversation.

'Desperate,' Dessie agreed, nodding in support.

'The market dictates everything, and yah know what? It's always right.' Jack raised his glass of beer and Bridie blushed.

'These things are cyclical,' Joyce said. 'The prices will drop again, but there are outside factors now that distort the market. We are under pressure regards interest rates, which totally dictate our lending criteria. People don't understand.'

I'd had enough. 'People do understand, Joyce, they aren't stupid. The banks own most of the housing stock, and the householder has little or no security until the mortgage is fully paid. You people could have a person evicted over very little cash. It's the truth, so what about the reckless lending?'

Joyce lifted her head, looking appealingly at Jack, who ignored her and drank all his beer.

'The banks were givin' the job by the state to house the masses,' I said. 'They were happy enough to do it for so long when times were good and profits were made but as soon as we hit a blip, it will stop – mark my words, it will stop.' I clapped once to emphasize my point and Bridie jumped in fright. 'They won't want to know, then the buck will be passed onto the state again, and what will the state do?' Everyone looked at me for words of wisdom but the wine had kicked in and wisdom was thin on the ground so all they got was, 'You'll see houses will be scarce, the state will have forgotten how to build them, and there will be wholesale mayhem – wait 'til you see.'

'Very dramatic, Kate,' Joyce said, 'but we will never go down that dreadful road. I can assure you that our banks won't allow that happen.' She was resolute, her right hand flat on the table in front of her flashing her mother's expensive rings.

Jack stood up at the head of the table. 'We should get another song from Bridie. Come on, you will?' He looked around. 'I'll tell yah what we will do – a noble call. I'll start us off. Go get yer guitar, Kate, and play along. Go on, young wan, or you're fired.'

I laughed. 'The guitar is in my bedroom, Jack. I might fall – I've had a glass too many.'

'You will play all the better so,' he said.

'I'll go get it,' Dessie offered. 'Is it on the bed, or have you hidden it away?'

'On the bed,' I told him, taking another sup of red wine, enjoying it more than before.

'I won't sing,' Joyce said. 'I haven't a note.' She seemed almost human.

'I'll sing so.' Dessie doused his fag in the huge ashtray, which resembled a flower vase.

Bridie laughed out loud as he sang" The town I loved so well" at the top of his voice, which was powerful but totally tuneless, and it didn't help that he forgot the words, having to stop twice and restart, much to Jack's amusement, his eyes watering with laughter.

Joyce was disgusted at Dessie's liberal use of the word "fuck" each time he had to restart, and Jack gave him a rousing reception, demanding an encore. We all laughed but Joyce put her hands over her face in horror.

Bridie sang another beautiful ballad, then recited a poem her father taught her as a child. It was stunning, and my tears threatened to overflow all the way through it. Dessie kept his head bowed and, for once, Jack didn't intervene or pass a critical comment. Even Joyce restrained herself as she looked on in begrudging admiration. She did sing in the end – a short, local song, as Gaelige, part of the Erris folklore she'd learned from the primary-school principal a few years back.

She went quiet after, and Jack finished off his wine, then gave us a rousing rendition of "The West's Awake", which succeeded in breaching the dam, sending hot tears down my cheeks. He got carried away with the emotion and the rest of us were deafened when he tried to hit high notes that just weren't reachable for him. They all thanked me for my humble guitar strumming and pleaded with me to sing a last song of the night while accompanying myself, so I sang the "Dangling Conversation" by Simon and Garfunkel. Dessie bowed his head for me, too, which was the greatest compliment he could pay. Bridie smiled at me all through, and Jack moved to sit beside Joyce. I almost stopped, as it seemed an unnatural thing to do, what with him ribbing her all day and night, but he put his arm around her shoulders – she didn't complain – and rested her head on his shoulder. She listened to my song with interest, then clapped the loudest in the end, her ever-present scowl replaced by a rare smile.

Bridie and Dessie were doing fine, with talk of him moving in with her. He was all excited about it and called by often to check on me and update me on his life.
'It will be somewhere for the kids to lay their heads. Bridie loves them and won't mind them comin' over, you know, as long as it's not every day, like.'
'That's decent of her.' I tried to sound positive. Their age difference always bothered me, for some reason.
'She's well used to kids. After rearin' her own, it's second nature.'

'Experienced,' I said, giving him a coffee.

'She has to go back to Cork for a little while,' he said.

'One of her daughters has mental issues – they think it's schizophrenia.'

'Oh, no.' I sounded far too worried, so I said, 'They can do wonders these days.'

'Yeah, it's her youngest, and she's very upset. She's leaving Angela in charge of the boutique.'

'She's her partner now, isn't she? She bought in?'

'She did, it's all good that way. I'd go with her but for the job, and Butlerstown is tiny – the gossips would love it.'

'Is Bridie worried about them?'

'Yeah, she mentioned it. But, sure, I know myself – it stands to reason.'

'I know, it would worry me, too, Dessie. Nothing as queer as folk.'

Bridie went home to care for her daughter, and she never came back. Her house in Flower Grove was sold, as was her share in the boutique, bought out by Angela. She never contacted Dessie to explain – it was Angela who told him that she had a man from Butlerstown waiting for her for years, who used to ring or write on a regular basis. Sometimes, he came to Dublin and visited the shop to take Bridie out. He was quite a bit older, and his wife had a terminal illness; once she passed, they were free to pursue their plans.

I expected Dessie to fall apart but he didn't. This time, he just went back to his bedsit, worked at his car selling, and had his kids at the weekends. Janet had a new boyfriend, with a reputation for being rough, and it drove Dessie mad as he was concerned for the kids. Bridie was gone now and he had to make do, so I didn't see him for ages. I was getting worried about him when he called by out of the blue, full of the joys of spring.

'Gilmartin wants me back. He's gonna give me my old job, car, and all. I can get out of that poxy flat and rent a proper house.'

'Great stuff, Dessie. You see, life goes on. Didn't I tell you that?'

'You did, Kate. It gets better, I have a date on Friday. Guess?'

'Who?'

'Guess?'

'I don't know, Angela from the shop?'

'Nah, do you give up?'

'Yeah, go on then.'

'Liz Cullen. I met her in Killiney Centre when I was getting a few things. Can you imagine?'

I couldn't hide my emotions, and my face must have told a million stories.

'Is that an issue, Kate?'

'Not at all, no, Dessie, you go see her, have a great night. It's just…we sort of fell out, and I got a bit of a shock when you said her name. Don't worry, I'm delighted for you.'

He accepted my explanation, though when he left, he was subdued.

After Mr Dazzle, I sought Liz out for advice but she brushed me away. She was so rude, it was like she'd never met me before, like I was encroaching on her space. I swore I would never engage with her again but now she'd found poor lonely Dessie – the bitch was rubbing it in.

12

'I think we should rob a bank.'

'What bank?' Dessie says.

'You know,' Kate answers, like she's asking him to pass the milk. 'Where Joyce used to work.'

'She's well gone now,' Dessie announces.

Kate nods to herself. 'She's dead. Her and Jack are both dead.'

Dessie is looking at the brown paper bag the blind man gave him. He picks it up from the sideboard. 'So we go in shootin', Kate, like in the movies, huh? Has Jack Oliver still got the imitation guns?' He takes the handgun from the bag and inspects it.

'In his cubbyhole.' Kate points to the padlocked press under the stairs where Jack Oliver kept his goodies. 'I always wanted to rob a bank, especially one that Joyce worked in – let's do it, Dessie, we can scatter the money all over the beach. Feed the gulls with cash.'

'We'd better get a plan then.' Dessie is serious. 'What's the plan?'

He puts the gun down and Kate searches for the key, which she finds in the top drawer of Jack Oliver's kitchen cabinet, holding it up in celebration. It is a big key, as keys go, and the padlock is big, too. She looks on sadly at Jack's wares: his fishing rod, lots of books, some outdoor clothing, his wellington boots, and a collection of replica guns that look as real as can be, including three handguns and a sub-machine gun.

Dessie laughs. 'He could start a mini war with this lot.'

'I miss Jack,' Kate says. 'Look, he has a few cases of wine too.'

'No use where he is, we might as well have them.'

'Sssh, don't disrespect the dead.' Kate beams at him and he smiles back at her.

She rang the hospital from her mobile, eventually getting through to the ward.

'You'd better come up, the doctor needs to see you,' the nurse said, her tone serious.

'Ok, I will be up within the hour.' Jael ended the call and checked the kitchen to see if Peter was still about, relieved to see that he'd gone back upstairs, most likely to sleep. She drank a mug of tea, before setting off on foot. It wasn't too far, just all a bit uphill, past the university apartments at Victoria Cross and on up the hill to CUH, where she found the ward easy enough and waited at the nurses' station for the doctor. Ten minutes turned into twenty, then a half an hour passed.

'Can I see my mum?' she said to a random nurse.

'She's sleeping,' she replied, like she was bothered at being questioned. She rushed off before Jael could ask where the doctor was and why she was kept waiting for so long.

After an hour, a clean-shaven fella arrived. He looked too young to be anything but introduced himself as the doctor. Jael thought he was nothing but then she saw that he had intense eyes that hinted at intelligence and integrity.

'You're her daughter? Jackie, is it?'

'No, my name is Jael – Jaelyn.'

'Oh, sorry, names are not my strong point. Listen, there isn't any easy way of saying this, but your mother has liver issues. Her liver is damaged, and she is really sick and is at risk. All we can do is try to put her on the program and give her hope.'

He never flinched as he delivered the words, and Jael looked at him, nodding – speechless.

He patted her shoulder. 'She may be well enough to go home for a few days, and we will see if they will take her on the program. But she is a drinker – I can see that – and to be honest, they are reluctant to take patients who keep drinking. It's important that she's willing to quit

*completely, to give it up, like now – today – or they won't
consider her for a transplant. The only positive here is that
she's young and that will count in her favour.'
He smiled and was about to go. 'You will have to tell her
all of that, as her daughter. It's no use coming from me.
Believe me, that's my experience.' He turned and left.
Jael sat back on her chair; her eyes full of tears.*

'A government that allows the spread of Covid because
money is bigger than health, deserves to have their pockets
picked.' Kate drinks her coffee and Dessie refills it with
hot water. He gives her another spoonful of granules.
He goes to the cooker where he resumes frying rashers and
buttering bread.
'They scared the shit out of everyone with Brexit, then it
was Covid, now back to Brexit, and they'll go back to
Covid again.' He looks at Kate to make sure she is paying
attention.
'If they had closed those dreadful Direct Provision centres
and regulated the Meat Factories, it would be a start,' Kate
says.
'Yeah, and allowing flights in from God knows where,
Kate. They're trying to protect the decimated public health
service they decimated, by the way.' He brings a plate of
buttered bread to the table.
'Yer spoiling me, Dessie, as always,' she says.
'Ah, sure, you deserve it.' He goes back to check the
rashers.
'It's the politics of reaction – they only react. Social media
is the new lobby, and the politicians run scared of it.' She
picks up a slice of bread.
After breakfast, she goes to her room and returns with two
masks. One is of Richard Fanon, the second is Michael
Ryan, the leader of the opposition. The masks are a good
likeness.
'Nobody steals like these politicians, hah?' she says.

Dessie laughs as he's washing up. When he's done, he goes over to Jack Oliver's cubbyhole and takes out one of the imitation handguns. He hands one to Kate, then takes the real weapon from the brown paper bag. With that, they set off in Kate's jeep.

The drive is warm, the sun is blinding. As they pass Elly Bay, children are kayaking. Dessie takes the twists and turns, then pulls in and parks in Brogan's car park. Several cars are parked nearby. A housewife runs back into the shop to get something she forgot, leaving her car engine ticking over. Dessie seizes the opportunity, and, in short time, they drive out with Kate beaming at the thought of adventure.

He finds a neat spot just down from the bank. They each put on a mask, with Kate choosing Richard Fanon and Dessie taking Michael Ryan. They walk unnoticed up the street and into the bank, where the teller laughs thinking it's a joke, as do some of her colleagues.

'Hand over the cash,' Dessie screams. 'Do it now. Fast! And no alarms if you know what's good for you.'

The teller is stunned and cowers beyond the Covid-glass partition. Dessie fires a shot into the ceiling, resulting in splinters of plaster falling to the floor. Kate is guarding the line of customers, who now have their hands in the air.

'Hand over the fucking cash.'

The teller complies, pushing wads of bank notes through the slot.

Dessie loads his carrier bag, which dangles from his shoulder. 'Give me fuckin' all of it,' he screams, then fires another shot at the ceiling. Some of the customers are now on the floor, covering their heads.

They exit the bank to return to the stolen car. He sets off as planned up the narrow road opposite. Kate watches as they pass a school, then fields and sporadic houses.

'Wow,' she exclaims, 'that's worth dyin' for.'

Dessie laughs. The fun begins when he looks back and
sees a car in pursuit. A passenger leans out the open
window and fires a pistol, sending sparks flying as the
bullets ping against the tar on the road.

*Attracta came home for a few days, and in that time, she
changed, showing humility.*

*'I can give it up,' she cried to Jael, 'but they say it might
be too late and I might need a new liver.'*

*Jael passed her a glass of water, and Attracta saw this as
a stay of execution on her road to catharsis.*

*'They won't consider me unless I quit – yer woman from
the team told me that.'*

*'You would ruin the new one just as quick,' Jael said, her
tone soft.*

*'Yah, I suppose.' Attracta looked odd without a proper
drink in her hand. 'I have a cocktail of drugs to take as
well.' She began to sob, her shoulders shaking.*

*'They'll keep you alive,' Jael said, rubbing her arm in an
effort to console.*

*'I was thinking, maybe we can get out of here, Jael. Maybe
we could go home.'*

'I dunno, we don't have a home – not anymore.'

*'We could find a place, you, and me. I could get better - I
don't know, get some work. I'll find something, and you
can work.'*

'You won't work again. Sorry, but you won't.'

*Attracta started to cry again. 'I wish I could turn back the
clock, you know. If I could, all would be so different, Jael,
I swear it would.'*

*'I know,' Jael said, brushing her mother's hair. 'I will get
us money, Mam, don't fret, I'm fit and able.'*

Dessie knows the back roads and finds his way back to the car park at Brogan's, leaving the stolen car back where they picked it up. Then they set off in the jeep, the holdall with the money safely in the boot.

'How much?' Kate asks, trying hard to be heard, her voice weak.

'A good few thousand,' he answers with confidence.

'Oh, what a waste,' she says. 'How many times in our lives did we really need money and we hadn't a dime?' She goes quiet, looking out the window. As the best of the day fades, the sea takes on a dark colour.

'Drive to the Atlantic side, Dessie, it looks like it's getting rough. I like it when it's rough.' She puts her hand on his thigh, and he jumps with surprise.

He drives up over the piles of stones laid to break storms, and onto the beach, the jeep skidding in the sand as he stops at the shoreline. Kate can barely open the door such is the power of the wind.

'Can you believe it, those bastards shot at us only because we were stealing the bank's money?'

Her words are the last she says in the interior of the jeep, her voice becoming a strained shout, the wind muting her no matter how much she tries to roar. Giant waves come crashing up to the jeep, and Dessie takes her in his arms and carries her out. She laughs and screams like a child, and he lets her down on the sand. She runs to the rear of the jeep and takes out the holdall, then they empty it, holding wads of notes in their folded arms. She fires her arms into the air, and the wind catches some bundles and they mix with the surf, while others land at her feet on the sand or are whipped away. Then she grasps several bundles and throws them into the waves.

Dessie is better. When his bundles fly into the air, the elastic bands snap and banknotes sail like small kites in the wind. Soon, notes dot the sky like seabirds.

'Fuck you!' he roars. 'Fuck your money, fuck you, fuck you.'

The fire keeps Kate warm and she nods off a few times. Dessie makes her soup and tries to give her bread, but she is exhausted from her day. She wants to tell him about her book and how she wrote about Jael's dream but is too embarrassed and wonders at the irony of it all. Sex with Richard Fanon and Peter is rape – it is dirty and perverted. In the dream, Jael had sex with Dessie – sensual and soft, skin on skin, and she feels emancipated in its wake. They make love as the huge waves engulf them, the salty sea rejuvenating them. Despite the age difference, he is a beautiful caring lover, and when he enters her, she scratches his back in deep lines, his blood under her fingernails. This sea cleanses it – disinfects the scourge of his wounds, and Jael is reincarnated.

'The night we went to Geesala,' Kate says, 'the little pub that had a bar shaped like a rowing boat, you, me, with Bridie and Jack, that was some night.'
'You were arguing about land ownership. I remember Jack was hopping mad. You were lucky he didn't sack yah.'
'He'd never sack me. If it weren't for me, he'd have gone to the wall. He was a good engineer, Dessie, but a lousy businessman.'
'Yeah, he told me you were indispensable, Kate.'
She goes quiet as she ponders his comments, remembering.
'So, developers buy up public land – remember, all land is public, no?' She eyes Jack.
'Not if some eejit buys it,' Jack says.
Dessie leans forward to hear Kate better, enthralled.
Bridie blushes.
'The eejit can't buy it, Jack, because we own it, it's not for sale.'

'Never heard the like.' Jack hammers back his wine but doesn't touch his dessert.

'If the citizen owns the land, Jack, it can't be bought or sold.'

He goes bright red in the face. 'Spit it out, Kate. What are you saying, woman?'

'The only cost should be the bricks and mortar – all else, we already own. Now, what will that do to the price of houses?'

She nods to herself. 'Ah, Jack didn't get me but, in fairness, Dessie, I think he'd go away and think about it. Like, the next day, he told me that he had a big think about what I said. Now he couldn't bring himself to agree with me but he thought about it just the same. Jack was like that, he was thoughtful, you know. He considered everything, like, from all angles. Jack was a clever man.' A sadness edges her voice.

Dessie gives her another cup of tea. 'I think I'll lay the head down,' he says.

She puts her tea on the side table and gives him a serious looks. 'Nah, sure, it's early yet, Dessie, it's not midnight.'

'I know but I get a terrible pain in my shoulder, right down my left arm. It goes after a good sleep but it's fuckin' bad today, Kate.'

'Will I rub it?'

'It's not that kind of pain – I'll sleep it off. Will yah be alright, yerself?'

'I will,' she says, her voice sad.

'Alright, night so.' He heads to his room.

Kate leans forward and stokes the fire. As usual, it brings thoughts fast and furious, the embers burning like little moments in time. She focuses, trying to piece them together to decipher one from another. She writes a letter to Jael.

Ah, Jael, I've had a sad life. No bones about it, and no point pretending it was anything else, either. People do that, you know, they make light of the big stuff – the tragedies that befall them. You shouldn't do that, Jael, you should tell the world what happened to your mother, and why it happened to her. Don't you see, love, that's why things never change because people like us, we don't speak out or tell the truth about stuff – the big stuff that destroys us, that puts us down and treats us bad, like. We must tell all, it's our duty.

Kate

Jael opened the hall door, worried when she saw the place in darkness. Peter was behind her, he went up three steps, using the light from his phone. She flooded the hall by turning on two switches, and Peter gave her a look but continued up his stairs like he was in a rush. The kitchen door was shut. She eased it open and turned on the light. Attracta sat in her favourite chair by the kitchen table, a glass of water in her hand, staring hard at the cooker opposite like she was checking if she'd left the gas on. Jael went closer, expecting her to pounce, saying something silly like "I got yah.", but she didn't, she just kept that intense stare. Jael knew – felt her cold – saw that she was angry that she'd died. Her death gaze gave it away.

13

Jael, I went to Dessie's room this morning, but he wasn't there. He has left with all his belongings, and his van has gone. Now it's just me. He did this before, you know, on that night he came to me and told me that Liz Cullen was only using him, having affairs behind his back. She opened up to him about me and Mr Dazzle, the abortion, and how Mr Dazzle's body was found later floating face down off Bug Rock. She was a traitor. Dessie was confused from what he felt was my deceit – no matter how much I tried to explain to him that I did it all to protect him, this fell on deaf ears – he was mortally offended by me, and totally inconsolable.

That night was the first time he mentioned his shoulder pain and the pain down his arm. I thought he'd hurt it, pulled a muscle, something simple like that. He got drunk and threw things in the scullery, breaking a few cups and plates. He was raging, and I ended up ringing a taxi, though he calmed down before he left.

I'll never forget it, Jael, the guard coming to my door a few days later. He was a big bruising country fellow. Told me that Dessie was dead, found in his bed by his landlord, who called to collect overdue rent. Dessie was dead in the bed, and he'd lain there for two days. I hadn't called him because I thought he was still pissed with me. Maybe he was, I never found out, as he never got to tell me how he felt when he went home to his lonely flat.

Sally and James were suitably subdued at his funeral, Sally more than James. Janet gave a "poor me" tear or two, but there was no sign of Bridie or Liz Cullen. Maybe she knew better.

Dessie left me all alone in the world. I eased my loneliness by reading books about Irish History. I read books on Mellows, Connolly, and true-life accounts of the counter revolution they call the civil war. That kept me busy.

Jack Oliver's family allow me stay here. I have come here so many times, down to the beach at Mullaghroe, over the Atlantic side, when I want the wind to blow the cobwebs out of my hot brain. This is my last visit here now, Jael. Dessie has left me so what's the point? The only thing he left behind was his gun – the blind man's gun. I'm reminded of all those years ago, us sitting in darkness in the caravan near Dunworley and Grandad reading from the Book of Judges…

Deborah, a prophetess and judge, advises Barak to mobilize the tribes of Naphtali and Zebulon on Mount Tabor to do battle against King Jabin of Canaan. Barak demurred, saying he would go, provided she would also. Deborah agreed but prophesied that the honour of defeating Jabin's army would then go to a woman. Jabin's army was led by Sisera. The armies met on the Plain of Esdraelon, where Sisera's iron-bound chariots became hampered by the mud after a downpour during the night that caused the Wadi Kishon to overflow its banks. The Canaanites were defeated and Sisera fled the scene.

Sisera arrived on foot at the tent of Heber on the plain of Zaanaim. Heber and his household were at peace with Jabin, the king of Canaan, who reigned in Hazor. Jael, however, sympathized with the Israelites because of the twenty-year period of harsh oppression inflicted on them by Jabin, his commander Sisera, and his nine hundred iron chariots. Jael (whose tent would have been separate from Heber's) welcomed Sisera into her tent and covered him with a blanket. As he was thirsty, she gave him a jug of

milk. Exhausted, Sisera lay down and soon fell asleep.
While he was sleeping, Jael took a mallet and drove a tent
peg into his temple, killing him instantly. The "Song of
Deborah" recounts:
Extolled above women be Jael,
Extolled above women in the tent.
He asked for water, she gave him milk.
She brought him cream in a lordly dish.
She stretched forth her hand to the nail,
Her right hand to the workman's hammer,
And she smote Sisera; she crushed his head,
She crashed through and transfixed his temples.

How I wanted to be Jael, to slay the oppressor Sisera
single handed – to feed him first, give him comfort, then
do the faithful deed. This is a massive breakthrough for
our sex, Jael, as they can beat us, rape us, ridicule us, but
we have the weapon of revenge. It is our final play, and we
have the tools to gain revenge, to make them pay for their
conquest of us. They have left the highways and byways,
those dark lanes to our souls, unsafe and insecure, and we
have only one weapon: our province, our revenge. You
take the gun, Jael, and you hold the honour, the life, and
soul of femininity within you.

Kate

Jael ran from the cottage, inhaling the country air, longing
for the freedom of the cattle in the field, the wild country
smell of dung cleansed by the salty air. She ran down the
laneway towards the main road.

Peter looked laboured. He should have been happy, with
the deals done and contracts signed. He'd sold his houses
to Richard Fanon and got his price too. But he still looked

worried, tense, and was rough with Jael – not physically but with his words and manner.

The taxi took ages to beat its way through the traffic. The more it rained, the slower they went, the coarser he got.

'This fuckin' city stops with a drop of rain.'

The taxi driver was Nigerian and didn't get the nuances.

'It rains very much here in Cork,' he said, trying to be friendly.

'Bet it buckets down in the jungle,' Peter said, and he wasn't joking.

The Nigerian smiled but didn't reply. He was quiet for a minute but then looked in his rear-view mirror. 'Too many one-way streets, this is your problem.'

Peter went to say something but snapped at Jael instead.

'You didn't put on the makeup he likes.'

'What?'

'The purple lipstick Richard likes you to wear. Put some on.'

The driver looked in his mirror. Jael reached into her handbag and took out the lipstick.

'Now,' she said when she was done, 'better?'

Peter looked away. 'Richard likes to be pleased.'

'What's the occasion?'

'A few party hacks. He wants to show you off, sweetheart.' There was no affection in his use of the term.

The club was darker than usual but they were later than normal. The music was loud, the clubbers in full flight, and pretty girls dominated the floor.

Peter escorted her to Fanon's office, where Richard was making gin and tonics for his guests, who all smiled at Jael when she walked in.

There were three of them, the oldest a greyish man who glanced at Richard and back at Jael. He wore an expensive suit, his face tanned like he'd spent time under a sun lamp.

'Gentlemen, this is the famous Jael.' Richard came from
his bar counter with a tray of gin and tonics. 'Peter?'
'I have things to do, Richard, I'll see you later.'
Richard smirked and Jael shivered but tried hard not to
betray any kind of fear or discomfort.
'Meet my friends, 'He waved towards a skinny man who
leaned on the arm of the couch. He had black eyebrows
but with the same face he sported as a child.
The man in the middle was dressed casually in a shirt and
trousers, and a neat leather Jacket. His hair was longer
than his two companions.
'Meet the future ministers.' Richard laughed, and all three
men joined in with him, but Jael didn't get the joke.
'Will you have a drink, Jael?' She shook her head. 'Oh, go
on, join the party. I'll get you some wine.' He returned to
the bar. 'All business associates of mine. I can't entice
them into politics, even with bribes and possible
ministerial appointments in time.' He laughed again as he
poured the wine. 'Says a lot for politics these days – so
hard to get quality to take part. No wonder we're left with
the dregs. Yes, we stumble ever downwards.' He was still
laughing at his own joke when he gave Jael her glass of
wine.

The laneway was long and winding and seemed to last
forever. She reached the main road, and a lorry passing at
speed created a vacuum that almost sucked her in. She
started to run; the sweat gathered in beads as she struggled
against the wind. The road was empty now and the fields
looked on eerily. She needed to drink from those isolated
troughs, she imagined cattle congregating, the wind
dusting the tufts of grass as they huddled, like they were
contemplating revolution.
She reached the entrance to the Atlantic beach, the sea
wind rushing in, gnawing its way over the rollers, up the
sands, and over the storm-barrier stones. Right then, it felt

like she was entering the mouth of a tiger, its horrific teeth finding flesh. At the end, at the water's edge, was Kate's Jeep. She kept running, looking out at the Inishkea islands far away, then the Hudson River and the New York skyline. The waves were bigger, crashing to the shore in temper. Kate sat there in the driver's seat, looking out, calm and dignified.

'Who would have thought it, Dessie dying like that? Thanks for bringing him to me, Jael, I meant to thank you before. You know that Liz Cullen? What a bitch. She did him in. She only wanted him to get at me. She did, I swear, and he, the eejit, couldn't see that. He didn't see that.

'I had a lousy life, Jael, a lousy life. I wonder, do many people have good lives, or are all our lives lousy, like? Does money make a difference? If you're loaded, is it different? You know, the biggest disservice they do to us is to remove our control. They want to control everything for us, and when the shit hits the fan, they act. Those people who get to call it, they only ever respond – their only brief is to seek popularity. That's their drug – their drug is approval, and they won't hand over the control because that's where the approval might actually mean something. Approval is always on the narrow levels, like on economy or on some warped sense of respectability. It's never on anything substantial.

'We have governments who get elected time and time again but they don't provide services for the electorate – that means either that most of the electorate don't need services or they do but don't realise they do. You know what, Jael, if you thought cancer wasn't bad enough, I think I have the Covid. Fucking sure I'd get it with yer man Richard Fanon on my TV giving me weather warnings, signing like I'm deaf, the Garda in uniform – he is warning me of Covid. I think I have it now.

'Wonder where I got it. Did you and Dessie pick it up from that kid in Direct Provision? It's in clusters where there are poor people – those slaves and disadvantaged people. I wonder, do they vote for a government that won't provide services to its citizens?

'People say I should have married. Yeah, maybe. If I'd married, Jael, I wouldn't be here on this beach, alone in the wind, the rollers breaking the fender on the Jeep. If I stay here long enough, I will drown. Saves on the gun.

'Do you know what the rumour was when I was young? They used to whisper but they were heard – those oul wans – thought we didn't hear them, but we did. They whispered that Grandad was touching me when Dessie was asleep. Touching me like I was his wife, like I was his property. I was twelve, Jael, only twelve. Grandad never laid a hand on me. Never. Whatever about his bible readings, his humours, his favourites, he never touched me, Jael, not once. They loved the filth – the filthier the better for some.

'I had a lousy life. It was lonely and frustrating. The ultimate sadness was going to Liverpool to be so alone. Make no mistake, girl, any woman who has relations with a man prostitutes herself, has always been the way of things, and it will remain so. Mrs Stubbs told me one night I stayed over, when Grandad brought Dessie to the hospital for his appendix, the oul bitch told me this parable about the field in the country where she lived, a small triangular field that was only any use for fat ponies or horses that were only fit for the knacker's yard. One night, she dreamed there were three men at one end: a banker, a politician, and a labourer, and at the other end, a girl barely sixteen, a fat woman in her fifties, and a married woman in her twenties, all standing naked in this field, the women in one corner, the men in the other.

'Days passed, and the distance between them was honoured. The men stayed in their corner down by the road, the women by the water trough up the steep hill by the hedge, 'til eventually the three men made their way up towards the women. The banker, who was the oldest of the men, showed an interest in the youngest girl, the politician chose the married woman in her twenties, and the labourer made for the fat woman in her fifties.

'Do you think the women refused them? Mrs Stubbs took delight in telling me that they didn't, as the field was their world, their only life. The men proceeded to engage the women, to force themselves on them, and the women accepted them as the field was their universe – there was no chance of another kind of life. So that was it according to the sad oul bitch.'

Tears flowed down Kate's cheeks, and she pushed her head back onto the headrest.

'I'm to end it here in this beloved place, with the Inishkea islands, and New York over the horizon. When Dessie was here, he'd think you could swim it, or walk it more like it – he said you'd go faster with the wind behind you. Aren't kids just fuckin' marvellous?'

She lifted the gun to the side of her head. 'Goodbye, cancer – goodbye, Covid.'

The blood spurted like a burst water main all over the seats, the ceiling, the windscreen, until Jael could no longer see her. She opened the jeep door, took the gun, and slipped it into her jacket pocket.

Each one of them took her in turn. Richard made a video, getting Jael to say things to the camera.
The men were a mixture. The first was softer, more considerate, than the other two. The skinny man was shy but rough because he didn't know any better. The oldest man was blunt and awkward he cursed regularly, shouting, "fuck," repeatedly. Richard gave them more drinks when it was done and sent Jael to his own private shower. She got dressed again and when she returned, the men had lost interest in her so she sat on her own by the

mini bar. While the men talked business and politics, she listened with a sharp focus.

When the men were leaving, Richard asked each of them for a donation, saying he was giving fifty himself – it was for the climax.

They all gave fifty.

'There you go,' he said, 'there's two hundred that Peter doesn't know about. You earned two hundred, you're a good girl.'

He put on his shades and escorted her out to the club. 'If you want to work for me regularly, I'll get you much more than that.'

She had to strain to hear him over the loud music. Then she spied Peter at the far side of the room talking to a young girl with a short skirt, who he then led away to a back room. Jael had to wait for him, her body sore, her legs hurting when she moved. When she sat on a high stool, the pain eased but only as long as she didn't move. Peter returned a while later, minus the girl, and in foul mood.

'Useless cunt,' he said, 'gone running home to Daddy.'

They got a taxi. Jael liked the city at night. It rained again; the drops thumped against the windscreen as they entered Washington Street. Late-night revellers sheltered in shopfronts, and two girls ran towards a red light and on across the road without looking.

The taxi driver was Irish and chatted to Peter about the economy, blaming the government. Peter nodded along, not mentioning that his new landlord was soon going to be a top politician. Jael noticed the election posters were soaked, with some slipping down the electricity poles. She wondered why the candidates all wore suits just like Ricard Fanon.

Jael called the doctor, who came an hour later. She offered her tea but the doctor refused. She was friendly but business-like.

'So, you found her like this?'

'Yes,' Jael said, her head bowed.

'She always sat there,' Peter offered, unperturbed, holding a neat whiskey. 'Couldn't move her,' he added. The doctor ignored him as she finished her examination.

'Right, Jael, we need to inform the coroner and the guards...and you will need to contact the undertakers.'

Jael cried like she'd never cried before, and the doctor comforted her. Peter left the room, whiskey in hand.

The white horses followed Jael 'til she reached the storm-barrier stones. When she glanced back, the sea was in around the jeep, the waves breaking on the windscreen. Back on the main road, she hitched a ride to Belmullet where she waited outside McDonald's pub for the bus.

14

*Six people attended Attracta's funeral service – Jael told
Peter that should he turn up, she would stab him to death
on the spot. Those who gathered were two fellow house
cleaners, and Mr and Mrs Scott, two tenants in another of
Peter's former properties, and a priest. As per
instructions, the whole service took place in Ringaskiddy.
Jael said a few words about Attracta, just about holding
herself together to speak. She wanted to thank Attracta for
all the good things she had brought to her life and was
relieved that her mother had a small life-insurance policy
that had just enough to pay the funeral costs. For once,
she could tell Peter to go fuck himself. He got the message
and made himself scarce.*

*'Attracta wasn't perfect but, who is? I'm not perfect,
either. We become the shape that life sets for us. There is a
giant we call God, and he moulds us through experience.
My mother, Attracta, was no different. Her own mother,
my gran Mary O'Dowd, she had problems with drink. It's
part of a dynasty, and my mother inherited it. She lived
with it, battled with it, beat it, then it beat her. When it did,
it devastated her. She would have to dig deep and start all
over.*
*'Many unkind people saw it as weakness. They thought she
was weak spirited. They thought she was lazy, that she
could be used and abused, even punished for her disease,
and it is a disease. Those people thought she had choices,
and that she made the wrong choices, but my mother
didn't have choices, just like her mother before her. She
was abused. She turned to alcohol, and the alcohol
relieved all and made her feel better about the world.
What she didn't see, and what her mother before her
didn't see, was that the relief was short-lived – the alcohol
was fooling them. It was to be their greatest abuser in the*

*end, but, my God, both my gran and Attracta were the two
kindest people I ever met – kinder than anyone and more
solid than anybody I know. Not a person can dispute this –
not one person.'*

*She broke down then, eyeing the framed photo of her
mother standing upright on the coffin. The tiny audience
clapped, and the funeral director signalled the pianist to
play "O Mio Babbino Caro". It was sung by this plump
lady who'd sat out of sight at the back throughout the
ceremony. The song was Attracta's favourite.*

There are just a handful of people on the bus: a few elderly
folk, and some student types wearing Covid masks. As it
crawls out of the town, the passengers gaze out at the
gloomy evening. Soon, they are approaching Bangor on
Erris, and Jael catches sight of the dark-blue waves of the
Glenamoy River as it runs naked alongside the road.
Beyond it is the desolate country of famished cows and
skinny foals, gaunt against the evening sky that is giving
up the day. She surveys the vast desert of infertile land all
the way to the horizon, 'til it disappears.

*'You will have to leave. I'll give yah a month. Look,
there'll be no more hanky panky – Richard said I wasn't to
touch you no more.'*

'Richard said,' Jael threw back at him.

*'He's my landlord now, don't yah see, Jael? Yar free of
him now, too – he found a new muse. By all accounts,
she's a cracker. If I, was you, I'd go to Dublin. Go back to
Dublin, get a job – there's lots of jobs for girls in Dublin.'*

*'So Richard doesn't need me, is that what yer saying,
Peter? Attracta dies and he doesn't want me anymore?'*

*'It's not that.' He sat at the far side of the kitchen table, on
Attracta's seat. He wasn't drunk. He wasn't drinking at
all.*

*'He's got a steady girlfriend – she's an actress. Well
known, too. But he's selling the club and will be in Dublin
most of the time now that he's elected. You might find
work with the new owners, Jael, but I don't know who it
will be. It might be safer to go back to Dublin. I might
head home myself; I don't want to be a tenant much
longer, you know. I'm used to being the man.'*
'I'm just a lump of meat to him?'
*He smiled at her. 'Jael, you know the score. He can't be
involved with girls anymore – he has to be "Mister
Respectability". The Party faithful will want him to be
squeaky clean or he'll never go up the ladder. Once he
tidies up his image, who knows where a good-looking fella
like him might end up.'*
*'He'll never be respectable. None of you will ever be
respectable.' She slammed the door and went to her room.*

The bus crawls through Crossmolina, and she's glad of the
neon – a break from the monotony of the dark countryside.
She passes a GAA stadium and looks out for the graveyard
but fails to find it. There are always graveyards in every
town and village, announcing to the world their humanity.
She falls asleep in Ballina and misses the journey from
Mayo into Roscommon: the dark villages, the ancient ruins
in lonely fields, the sad oasis under overhanging trees;
small groves where, in daylight, lovers meet. She misses
the purring sound of the engine as it speeds up on the good
stretches of road, soon to fade when they become twisty
near Frenchpark, then all the way to Strokestown, with its
wide main street empty of humans but still boasting of
commerce with prominent banks.

*Richard is making another drink for himself. Jael is
unafraid, as he isn't drunk, though his attitude has
changed a little – the hostility and bullying have
dissipated.*

'I'm sorry for your loss, Jael. If there's anything I can do? Like, if you need money, I can write you a cheque. How much do you need to get you started again?'

'I don't need money, Richard, not your money.'

'It's a gift for the work you did here.' He swallows his gin.

'I didn't work here, but you paid me anyhow. If you call that night work, you have a problem.'

He sits on the couch, and while the smirk still stains his face, he looks worried.

'So why did you come to see me? Like, you know what's happening, I know Peter spoke to you. I'm moving on, Jael. I'm a TD now. I'm no longer the owner of a night club – I have to grow up and change my ways. If that means apologising to you, well, yeah, I'm sorry, I shouldn't have done those things to you, I shouldn't have said the things I said to you. I'm been honest now. And I destroyed the video tape. I watched it a few times but I destroyed it out the back in the incinerator bin. It's gone forever, Jael – it's the least you deserve. Once again, I apologise to you. Look, let me write you a cheque in settlement for any distress I caused you. We can call it quits with my apology. You can move on and I can form new relationships without all of this weighing me down. To be honest, Jael, I don't know what got into me. It's like I had some kind of event – I just wasn't me for a long while.'

His smirk enlarges to cover his whole face. He's on his feet again, heading towards the mini- bar. When he gets around to the rear, he opens a drawer and takes out a large chequebook. 'How much, Jael? How much is my apology worth? Like, once we agree, we should never mention what happened in here again, is that clear?'

There's a hint of harshness in his tone but he physically softens and smiles. 'I didn't offer you wine. Will you have some wine?'

'No,' she says.

He comes back around the mini bar, his large chequebook flapping in his hand. 'I will go to two grand. That will set you up, if you go back to Dublin, and you agree that it's over and not to be mentioned it again. How's that?'

She stares at him, seeing how uncomfortable he is – his right foot moving involuntarily, his chin quivering. 'I dunno, Richard, you humiliated me, and my mother. The prices in Dublin are crazy, and you are fucking nasty. Might be impossible to get a place, a cheap place, I mean. You go write me a cheque for five grand and I will take yer apologies seriously. Let's say it's two and a half for me and two and a half for Attracta.'

'You drive a hard bargain but I can't go over three grand. That's fifteen hundred each. I will speak to a few friends about getting you reduced rented accommodation in Dublin. How is that?' He drinks his gin down like he's on a victory parade.

'No, it's five grand, Richard, or I call the press and tell them what a scumbag you really are.'

His face hardens, turning red. He goes to approach her but stops half-way. Jael can see that he's thinking about something.

'You know Tony and Jim? If I call them, you will end up in the Lee, and neither of us will have to worry about all this again. I can pick up the phone – they might even want to have a bit of fun with you first. How's that, Jael? Don't be bursting my balls now, I'm trying to be straight with you but you are antagonising me.' He throws his gin glass against the far wall and it smashes to pieces. His face is bursting. 'Do you want to end up in the river?' He's holding his forehead, like he has a terrible headache.

'No, but you want me to go away and forget.' She grips the back of his office chair as the room tilts. 'If you kill me, it will come out – you will have to kill Tony, and Jim too. They could blackmail you, Richard. You will be

blackmailed. The sensible thing is to give me the money
and let me go. You will never see me again.'
He composes himself and looks her up and down. She
doesn't flinch. 'Ok, how about I give you five grand but I
keep an interest in you? You come see me the odd time
when I'm overnight in Dublin. I might make a deal like
that.'
'You're sick.'
'No, I'm just keeping you close, Jael. If the press get wind
of it, it's current, like I'm dating or even having an affair,
and they'll stick to the unwritten politicians code of
honour, but old stuff with a schoolgirl, just isn't covered. I
will give you lots more in time if you agree – expensive
dinners in top restaurants, the best drinks in top clubs, a
lovely apartment courtesy of one of my pals. How about
that, Jael?'

The bus stops in Longford for a break and some
passengers get off to get takeout food and use the toilets.
Jael needs to pee but waits 'til the other passengers have
left. When she gets off, the night air is cool and she
realises that she's hungry. She didn't think Longford was
such a big town. She gets a Supermacs and uses the loo
she is last getting back on. They set off into the lights of
the oncoming traffic, and more faceless fields await.
The bus goes through Mullingar and two elderly people
get off, removing their masks once they're outside. The
Dublin road is getting shorter, and as they pass into
Kildare, the countryside lights up; the streetlamps
beaming. They pass through Lucan, headed for the city.

Richard Fanon is addressing a Party rally in the conference
centre, that iconic building that reminds Jael of a child
playing with building blocks. His security at the door
ignore her as she enters. She's wearing her mask, with
only her eyes visible. Most of the crowd are leaving, and

people brush by her, all wearing rosettes, the men in suits, with well-dressed women in the main. She goes up two floors, where the after-rally party has finished, and cleaning staff are vacuuming around the floor and cleaning the tables. Some stragglers are still supping champagne from plastic cups. She sees Richard standing with two men in the distance, in deep discussion. There are large campaign photos of him all over the room. She removes her mask and stuffs it into her pocket.

'I wondered how far you would go, Richard. Never this far. You know I won't bother going to the press, you're not worth it. You can inflict yourself on politics, on the poor duped eejits in this country, but you won't touch me again, not ever. And don't bother with your cheque, either I would spit on it and throw it in the river. Let's hope we don't meet again – ever.'

Before she knows it, both bodyguards Tony and Jim grab an arm.
'Jael,' Richard shouts, like he's found a long-lost friend. He leaves the discussion to come over. 'Alright, lads, we won't ruin the night. Jael, surprised to see you. Were you here earlier? I didn't see you.'
'I came to talk to you, Richard, about stuff you know.'
'Come on, there's a room – it's off here.'
Tony and Jim go to follow but he stops them with a wave of his hand. 'It's ok.'
Tony shrugs and Jim looks pissed off but they both obey.
'What is it, Jael? I hope you didn't come to spoil my big night – there's an after party in my friend's apartment. You could do yourself up and come along – no problem, I'll organise it.'
'I hear you're going for Party leader.'
'Yes, after tonight. I have it, though the vote is not 'til next week – but I'm confident.' That smirk spreads across his

face. 'It's been quite a rise. First a minister, now the possible leader. Well, let's say leader – might as well be confident. Did you hear the things they were saying about me? My God, there's this rumour doing the rounds that I'm gay. Me, gay? Could you credit that?'

Jael takes the gun from her pocket and aims it at his forehead. He is no more than three feet away, his eyes wide, glancing at the closed door, then at the ashtray full of cigarette butts. Someone has inexplicably left orange peels to mix with the ash.

'What's this, Jael? Are you still sore?' He glances again at the door.

She squeezes the trigger, and the gun kicks up. The shot is very loud and she almost falls backwards. Richard is still looking at her, his eyes frozen, blood oozing from a hole in the middle of his forehead. Then he crumples forward, as if to hug her, and she can't move back fast enough to stop his blood smearing her face and hair, and as he collapses to the floor, the front of her blue jeans turns red. Without looking at him, she returns the gun to her coat and walks out the door.

Tony and Jim rush by her but she continues walking at the same pace, through a crowd that has gathered to investigate the loud bang. She's on the escalator going down when she hears voices shouting, 'Stop her! Stop her!'

She puts her mask back on and walks out into the darkness to the comforting sound of Liffey flow.

The bus to Cork is not as interesting – there are no rivers or views of desolation. The driver plays the news on the radio – it's all about the killing of Richard Fanon. She guessed right, there isn't any description of her, the news declaring that the Gardaí are seeking witnesses and the suspect was a female in her late teens, early twenties. Taking those ten minutes to wash and rinse in the toilet of

the late-night bar was a sound decision. The gamble on the
Party shutting it all down is a good one – both Tony and
Jim know her well but they will be bought off for the sake
of the Party's reputation. In many ways, the powers that be
are taking a gamble, too, that she won't go to the media,
which, of course, she won't. In this game, the gamblers
win.

The journey revives her as she looks over rich farmland,
with herds of quality cattle and strong thoroughbreds in
Tipperary, with the high Galtee's marking the gateway to
Cork. She thinks of Dessie, the drive into the abyss. Above
the mountains the turbulent flow of the Bandon river. It
covers the taillights of random cars with its mix of black
and dirty brown. In its infinite cascade of light, and dark,
over slender rocks, gushing through false gullies. In this
frenzy hailstones fall hard without mercy. The wipers
going at supersonic speed, and the heat blower on full, still
she couldn't see in front of her. Dessie his bald head
touching the windscreen it is cold against his skin, for a
moment, he is a mannequin a crash test dummy. The sky
lights up, and there is an almighty blast of thunder before
the rain gets worse. A single battered tree lies submerged
in the semi dark river flow. The river swishes onto the
road and Dessie slows the van, like a small boat, it floats
westward towards the great falls.

At last, the bus comes to a stop at Parnell station. She
walks along the quays and stops to check out an
unflattering poster of Richard Fanon – some kids drew a
moustache on him and wrote "Gay" beside his face. When
she's further up the street, she notices that people are
staring at her, and remembers the dried blood on her jeans.
She goes into a clothes' store and buys new jeans, stuffing
the old ones in the new bag, then continues up Washington
Street, passing UCC. She uses her old key, makes a strong

cup of tea, and eats some cream crackers that were still in their pack unopened.

She stops at the top of the stairs, slightly breathless after the steep climb, then knocks on Peter's door. He doesn't answer so she turns to leave but notices that it's not locked, so she presses on it and steps in. Standing there in the silence, she wonders if Peter is gone out but then hears a soft cry from the bedroom. She walks to the bedroom door and it creaks open. A young girl, no more than sixteen, is straddling him. She is thin, with jet-black hair, and wearing too much makeup. The girl sees her first and screams, then Peter's head pops up, his eyes wide open. 'What dah fuck?'

'Go!' Jael shouts to the girl. 'Go.'

The girl moves smartly off the bed and puts her clothes on double quick. 'You said you weren't married,' she screams at Peter, who is still trying to figure out the whole thing. 'What the fuck, Jael?' He glances at the girl, looks back at Jael, then pulls the covers back, exposing his erect penis. 'Want some?' He smiles, moving his eyebrows up and down.

Jael hears the girl go out the front door, slamming it behind her.

She takes the gun out and Peter pulls the blankets up to his chest, his eyes like saucers. 'It was you. It was fuckin' you that shot him. You fuckin' crazy bitch.'

The bullet enters his forehead, and a single red spot on his pillow seeps red. Jael stays to look at him, at the shock on his face. She smiles and lays the gun on the bottom of his bed.

The rain lashes down on the Western Road and dark pools form by the bus stop. Passing traffic sends water swishing, flowing over the kerb and over her shoes. She wears a short skirt; she is doused with makeup. The rain is bad for business but it doesn't stop it. She has learned in the real world that nothing stops business – money keeps on turning, just like the globe spins on its axis. A jeep pulls in and she speaks to the driver, who she can hardly hear with the pounding rain and the sound of the wipers. The repetitive noise is unsettling, reminding her of someone from a different time. She climbs into the jeep, and it eases away to join the line of traffic.

The End

Clear-View Editing @eamonocleirigh
Jan 18
Irish writer Paul Kestell's new work is a powerful write, with challenging themes that will hit you where it smarts. It is relatively short but packs a punch above its weight.

Printed in Poland
by Amazon Fulfillment
Poland Sp. z o.o., Wrocław

24412413R00079